ADVANCE REVIEWS

"Elise Faulkner drew me into her head and heart so subtly, yet with such force, that by the end I was cheering her on. Suzanne Kamata has woven an honest, aching coming-of-age story that will speak to women everywhere."

KRISTIN BAIR O'KEEFFE
Author of *The Art of Floating* and *Thirsty*

"Suzanne Kamata has written a novel of great charm and depth, with a bit of magical realism laced with humor. Elise, its engaging narrator opens her arms and her heart to life's complexity, including family secrets and escapades with a magnificent new bestie—the irrepressible Chiara. When an unlikely romance unfolds with a mysterious drifter/musician, Kamata steers us expertly into darker waters. A jewel of a novel, set on the shores of Lake Michigan with Kamata's signature compassion for all of its characters."

MARGARET WILLEY
Winner of the Gwen Frostic Award and
Author of *Summer of the Silk Moths*

". . . a beautiful story about a teenage girl who must learn to balance her idealism and belief in mermaids with the harsh realities of growing up and trying to find people to love and trust. A page-turner set in the unstable years of the 1970s, it brought back memories of my own adolescence and took me beyond, in that way all good novels do, into the wonderings of circumstance and the choices we would make if faced with hard decisions. Suitable for teens and adults alike, this novel will teach readers to believe in magic even in the face of tragedy."

CASSIE PREMO STEE
Author of *Beautiful Wat*

D0911532

THE MERMAIDS OF LAKE MICHIGAN

a novel

THE MERMAIDS OF LAKE MICHIGAN

a novel

SUZANNE KAMATA

Wyatt-MacKenzie Publishing
DEADWOOD, OREGON

ALSO BY SUZANNE KAMATA

Screaming Divas

Gadget Girl: The Art of Being Invisible

The Beautiful One Has Come: Stories

Call Me Okaasan: Adventures in Multicultural Mothering

Losing Kei

Love You to Pieces: Creative Writers on Raising a Child with Special Needs

The Broken Bridge: Fiction from Expatriates in Literary Japan

The Mermaids of Lake Michigan
Suzanne Kamata

ISBN: 978-1-942545-59-0

Library of Congress Control Number: 2016951990

Excerpt from from "Mermaid's Love"© Leza Lowitz. Reprinted with
permission of the author and Wandering Mind Books.

Oil painting on cover "Transcendence" © Erika Craig.
Used with permission. www.erikacraig.com

Photo of Chicago Skyline © Halbergman | iStock by Getty Images

Wyatt-MacKenzie Publishing
DEADWOOD, OREGON

Wyatt-MacKenzie Publishing, Inc.
www.WyattMacKenzie.com
Contact us: info@wyattmackenzie.com

D E D I C A T I O N

In memory of my grandmothers Frances Mund and Edith Linn,
each amazing in her own way.

"There were no princes. It was simple. Rocks
on the shore were heavy. Our bodies had weight.
We were clumsy. Everywhere we looked love found
us watching; love was a shape-shifter, glow-in-
the-dark star I stuck on the ceiling of a blue
heron sky."

LEZA LOWITZ
from "Mermaid's Love"

ACKNOWLEDGEMENTS

A big thanks to Peter Carey, who oversaw the writing of an early draft of this novel through the Humber College School of Writers; the late Carol Houck Smith, who told me that I was starting this novel in the wrong place (she was right!); early readers Helene Dunbar, Chris Tower, and Eric Madeen for feedback; the editors of *The Heartlands Today*, for publishing an excerpt; Amanda Hurley and Jotham Burrello of Elephant Rock Books for recognition and encouragement; Nancy Cleary for loving this story as much as I do and bringing it to life; Karen Kibler for copyediting; Carrie Pestritto for deal-making and support; Team CaPes (you know who you are) for cheerleading; Kristina Riggle, Cassie Premo Steele, Kristin Bair O'Keefe, and Margaret Willey for kind words; Leza Lowitz for the poem excerpted at the beginning of this book; and Erika Craig for lending her gorgeous painting for the cover.

I am also indebted to a number of authors whose works I consulted in crafting this story. *Bury Me Standing: The Gypsies and Their Journey* by Isabel Fonseca and *Lola's Luck: My Life Among the California Gypsies* by Carol Miller were especially helpful in deepening my understanding of Rom culture. The folktale in chapter sixteen is from *Gypsy Folktales* by

Diane Tong. In creating Elise's great-grandmother, I borrowed heavily from the biographical sketches of real-life wreck divers Margaret Goodman and Frances Baker in the wonderful anthology *The Women's Great Lakes Reader* edited by Victoria Brehm.

I am grateful for the enduring support of my family. Thank you, especially, Yukiyoshi, Jio, Lilia, Mom, Dad, Tim, Kavita, and Yukiyo.

And finally, to all who buy, sell, read, and review this book, none of this is possible without you! Thank you!

THE MERMAIDS OF
LAKE MICHIGAN

1

If I had to declare the exact moment my life changed forever, I'd name a steamy July afternoon in my seventeenth year. It was a week after my little sister Amanda made her debut with the Grand Rapids Junior Ballet, and two weeks before the beginning of the carnival. I was holed up in my room, deeply engrossed in *The Blood of Others*, overcome by the tragic love of French Resistance fighters. Bullets were whizzing about my head. There might have been a soundtrack, too—violins or the plaint of piano keys. I was caught up in the danger, the secrecy, the romance. Ooh, la la.

There was a knock on the door. I knew it was Mom. Amanda usually barged right in. Besides, she was still at her ballet lesson.

"What?" I called out, hoping my voice held the right note of irritation.

Mom opened the door and stepped into my room. I didn't look at her, but I figured she was taking stock of the clothes lying in soft piles on the floor.

"Mrs. Churchill just called to invite you over for tea," she said. "She wants you to meet her granddaughter who's visiting for a while."

Mrs. Churchill was the widow who lived a few houses down and across the street from ours. These days I rarely saw her, and to me her life was as far away from mine as the moon is from earth. Mom, however, considered her a friend. They went to Bible study together at the Methodist church, and sometimes Mom brought her a loaf of freshly baked bread or a jar of homemade dill pickles.

I kept my eyes focused on the book in front of me. "Tell her thanks, but no thanks. I'm extremely busy with various activities."

"Her name is Chiara. She's the same age as you. In fact, you might be in some classes together this fall. It looks like she'll be going to school here."

"Sorry."

Mom couldn't understand why Amanda was always getting phone calls and party invitations while I was spending my summer vacation in my room, reading. Early on, she had designated herself a matchmaker of sorts, my own personal friend-finder.

At the age of twelve, my best friend was a girl named Fabrice Nwanko who lived in a village in Ghana. We'd never met face to face, although we had exchanged pictures. Fabrice had chocolate skin and wiry pigtails and wore a navy school uniform. In my mind, she was always dressed like this. Our friendship consisted of letters—rather breathless accounts of imagined deeds on my part, interspersed with small doses of reality. Fabrice, who was taught by missionaries, wrote in schoolgirl script, her letters always neat and legible.

I made her acquaintance through an advertisement in the back of a magazine for girls. Her name and address were listed under the heading "Pen Pals Wanted." According to Fabrice, I was the only one to answer her ad. Probably other girls were put off by the difficult spelling of her name, but I was attracted by its exoticism.

I had other pen pals as well—Fatima in Algeria who

had a pet camel named Olga, Keiko in Japan who always mixed up her ls and rs ("My family works in a lice field"), and Jenny who lived in Pennsylvania.

Fabrice often asked for presents—a camera for her father, watches, American dolls. I wondered if the missionaries encouraged her to ask for these things or if I'd somehow given the impression that I was from a wealthy family. (Had I written to Fatima that we had five bathrooms in our house, or was that to Fabrice?) The truth was that I received a modest allowance each week—hardly enough to buy a few candy bars.

I couldn't afford the things Fabrice wanted, but I didn't want to do without her letters.

"Dear Elise," she wrote, "my uncle was down at the beach one night not long ago and he saw a mami-wata. She sat in the shallow water, swishing her tail and calling out in a voice as sweet as honey. Uncle couldn't resist. He promised to love her forever and he has been a little crazy ever since. Beware of mermaids."

See, I had a thing about mermaids. I couldn't do without her stories and so I, too, made promises—of cameras, dolls, all the riches of the Western world—just to make sure those letters kept coming.

I spent so much time writing to my faraway friends that I had none left over for the kids in the neighborhood. It didn't matter much to me. Their houses were not as interesting as Fatima's with its tiled walls and pool-sized bath tub. Their pets were boring compared to Fatima's camel. And not one of them had seen a mermaid.

"Why don't you invite that Kristy Evans over?" Mom had said one afternoon.

"Can't," I said. "I have to write to Fabrice."

She rolled her eyes toward the ceiling. "Fatima, Fabrice, Fatima. That's all I ever hear. Do these girls actually exist?"

I pulled open the bottom drawer of my desk. All the letters I'd received were stored there. I reached in and fished out an envelope made of flimsy blue paper. "Do you know what Fatima said in her last letter? She has to start wearing a veil whenever she leaves the house so men won't get excited from looking at her. Isn't that weird?"

"Yes, very weird." Mom sounded exhausted. "But don't you want to get together with other kids your age? Don't you want to have slumber parties and go roller-skating?"

"No," I said. "Not really."

But then Fabrice, who is three years older than I am, wrote to say that she was getting married, and her letters became fewer and fewer. By the time Mom marched into my room with news of Mrs. Churchill's granddaughter, I hadn't heard from her in two years.

During Mom's last all-out campaign a couple years before, she had persuaded me to join the youth group at church.

"It'll be fun," she said. "They have hayrides and dances. You might meet some nice boy and fall in love."

I had my doubts, but I indulged her. I joined the group.

Mrs. Gibbons, the adult leader, was also director of the bell choir. Her eyes were magnified by the thick lenses of her glasses and her rusty hair was perpetually frizzy. In her dour presence we read Bible verses and discussed inspirational tracts and what to do about "teen problems."

"What if someone offers you a can of beer?" Mrs. Gibbons asked on one occasion. There were smirks all around which she somehow failed to see. Finally, Mindy Anderson spoke up. "Just say no." She was so pure that she buttoned her polo shirts all the way to the top.

We planned bake sales and car washes and afternoon dances. But as soon as Mrs. Gibbons left the room to prepare refreshments or take a phone call, the other kids would start telling dirty jokes. They were disgusting, really. Paul, the minister's son, was the worst. He used words that had never passed my lips. I was confused. Weren't we supposed to be thinking about God?

The last straw came when we were in the middle of a treasure hunt. We were searching for a chalice with the aid of clues scribbled on paper. I read my hint: "Sing Hosannah from the highest!" Easy. I climbed straight to the choir loft. There I found Paul and Mindy, horizontal on the front pew. His hand was tunneling under Mindy's floral skirt and they were both panting.

All of my illusions about youth fellowship were shattered. Mom's would have been as well, but I never told her exactly why I quit. But I vowed then and there that I would never let her push me into a similar situation. And now here was my mother, Miss Coast Guard USA 1963, standing in the doorway, tapping her foot in three-quarter time. I finally looked away from the book.

"I've already told her that you'll go. She's expecting you tomorrow afternoon at three."

I gritted my teeth. "Mom, did it ever occur to you that I might be busy tomorrow? That I might have plans?"

"Well, no. You go to the pool, and then you stay cooped up in your room until dinnertime."

"Maybe I want to finish this book," I said. "Did you ever think about that?"

She pressed her forehead with the palm of her hand as if I were giving her a migraine. "Fine. I'll call Mrs. Churchill right now and tell her that you can't come because you're impossibly asocial and you'll be reading. But let me just say one thing. You may be missing out on something. An opportunity." And with that, she turned and stormed off down the hall without bothering to close my bedroom door.

"Oh, hell," I muttered under my breath. Maybe it wouldn't be so bad. Plus, the idea of "tea" was just quaint enough to seem interesting. Who ever had "tea" in Grand Haven, Michigan? It was something out of a regency romance novel. I wondered if there would be crumpets. And frankly, I was feeling a bit lonely.

"All right," I yelled. "I'll go."

Mom didn't answer, but she didn't pick up the phone either. I would be at Mrs. Churchill's on time.

2

I'd actually met Mrs. Churchill's granddaughter once before, on the day I turned five, at the Coast Guard Festival parade.

I remembered how, in the days leading up to my birthday, Amanda and I had ridden along in the station wagon when Mom went to pay the bills, cruising past the waterfront where the components of carnival rides were strewn across a parched lot like giant Erector Set pieces. I saw the gondolas that would soon dangle from the top of the Ferris wheel, the tent poles that would support canvas awnings over the ring toss game, and the carousel horses painted with garlands, napping on the crisp dried grass. I knew it was only a matter of time.

"Mom," I called out from the back seat. "How many more days 'til I turn five?"

She turned the car into the electric company parking lot. "Eight days, sweetie."

The carnival opened on a Friday night. Mom promised that as soon as Dad came home we would go together. Amanda had little memory of the previous year's festival, but I recalled that she had been frightened by the crowd. I was looking forward to munching on corn dogs and candy apples. This year, I promised myself, I wouldn't cry when I went into the haunted house.

Mom had us bathed and dressed in matching sailor dresses and bloomers by the time Dad came home. He stepped in the door and kissed Mom. "I got caught in traffic again. All those tourists!"

During the festival, the town was swarming with people we had never seen before, people who drove cars with different-colored license plates and who sometimes spoke foreign languages. Just that afternoon, I'd seen a dark-skinned man with his head wrapped in cloth. The woman with him had a red dot on her forehead and a huge scarf draped across her body. I knew that they must have come from very far away.

Dad sank into his Naugahyde recliner, took off his glasses, and pinched the bridge of his nose.

I rushed over and tugged at his sleeve. "Daddy, come on! We're going to be late."

Amanda tried to climb onto his legs.

"Jim," Mom said softly, "the girls are hungry." She was holding her purse and standing near the door, ready to hop into the car. I knew she was looking forward to the carnival, too.

Finally, Dad sighed, put his glasses back on, and eased himself out of the chair. After he'd changed out of his work clothes and into plaid Bermuda shorts and a white T-shirt, we set out for that once-a-year wonderland.

The carnival lasted for a week, the duration of the festival, and was open from morning to midnight. After that first evening when we'd ridden the merry-go-round until our heads spun and gorged on cotton candy till our tummies bulged with pink stuffing, we begged to go every day, but Dad grumbled something about money and trees.

Mom pulled us onto her lap. "The carnival is very special, but if we went every day we wouldn't think so anymore. Its magic would disappear."

Although I was disappointed, I pretended to understand and let myself be pacified by a game of Old Maid.
There was still one more thing to look forward to.

The annual parade started at the center of town,
then snaked down Main Street past the grassy park with
the gurgling fountain, past Steketee's department store
where Mom bought our dresses, and all the way down to
the banks of the Grand River where it flowed into Lake
Michigan. But before that, Dad took us on tours of Coast
Guard cutters moored in the harbor.

I was intimidated by the men in crisp white uniforms, and I didn't understand the dials and gauges. I let
my mind wander, imagining that I was a mermaid
plucked from the sea by a band of pirates and I had to
find a way to escape. While my head was busy with this
story, my feet took me through the hulls and corridors
in the wake of my father's footsteps.

The rest of the time, I was counting down. I would
eat five, four, three more bowls of Rice Krispies before
my birthday came. I would brush my teeth ten...eight...
six more times. I would watch this many more "Bullwinkle" and "Underdog" cartoons, take this many more afternoon naps. And then, finally, I woke up one morning
and robins were tugging worms from the lawn and the
dewy grass sparkled in the sun, and I knew that I was five.
I pushed back the covers, jumped out of bed, and threw
the door open, ready to embrace all the wonders of the
day.

"Happy birthday, Princess," Dad said. It was Saturday, so he was home, sitting in his recliner, skinny hairy
legs sticking out of his shorts.

On my birthday I got the royal treatment. Mom
made my favorite breakfast—a scrambled egg sandwich
with lots of mayonnaise smeared on the bread. I got to

wear new clothes—a dotted Swiss pinafore sent by Grandpa and Grandma. And later, of course, there would be presents and a cake, maybe in the shape of an animal or a heart, and everyone would sing to me.

The parade, which I couldn't help thinking would be held in my honor, was at ten o'clock. In the evening, there would be a show of the musical fountain ("The World's Largest Musical Fountain!") followed by fireworks.

By the time we got to Main Street, the sidewalks were already thronged with spectators. Some people had set up lawn chairs and coolers filled with ice and canned soft drinks. We brought an old Army blanket which Dad spread on the grass by the curb. I knew that if I couldn't see, Dad would hoist me onto his shoulders for a better view, but now that I was a big girl of five, I wanted to stay on the ground on my own two feet. Mom hadn't packed any treats for us because there was always someone wheeling a little white cart of ice cream bars and popsicles. We loved to go dashing after the vendors with quarters clutched in our fists.

"Julia Bremer, is that you?" A plump woman in a broad straw hat stepped up to Mom. She looked old enough to be a grandmother.

"Oh, hello, Mrs. Dudley," Mom said. "I'm Julia Faulkner now."

The woman moved in and gripped Mom's hand. "You still look so pretty," she gushed. "I remember when you were in the parade. I even remember that blue gown you wore. Satin, wasn't it? Seems like yesterday. And who do we have here? Are these your little angels?" She peered at us from under the brim of that hat and reached out to pat our heads. "Darling girls. Absolutely darling. Maybe we'll see them riding down Main Street one day." And then she was off down the street.

In that small town, Mom was almost as famous as Droopy, the clown, who made an appearance at every parade and high school football game. I was proud of her, but when I looked up, I saw that her eyes were glazed over like Dad's when he was watching sports on TV. She stared into space until a gloved hand tapped her shoulder.

It was Mrs. Churchill. She was the only person I'd ever seen with a parasol. She held it in one hand. With the other, she was hanging onto the fingers of a girl about my age with hair the color of orange Kool-Aid. I wanted to take a pen and connect the freckles on her face into funny constellations.

"Here you are, Julia," Mrs. Churchill said. "I've got my daughter's girl with me for a few days." Then she whispered, but I heard, "Another d-i-v-o-r-c-e."

Mom murmured words of sympathy and fluttered her fingers as they moved on through the throng. Then her eyes went back to Main Street.

I looked after the girl with the flaming hair, not knowing that she would one day explode into my life again. I watched her 'til she was eclipsed by a family in matching seersucker outfits. Then I forgot about her for a long time.

The parade was coming. First came the high school marching band in their navy and gold uniforms, knees lifting in unison. Then came the baton twirlers, little girls in sequins and smiles, only a few years older than I. I craved their glamor, envied them their white rubber-tipped wands. I watched them twirl and toss until my attention was snagged by the Shriners in red fezzes driving miniature cars.

Dad lifted Amanda onto his shoulders, and I slipped my hand into Mom's. I wanted to somehow convey my perfect happiness and to share it with her. She squeezed

my hand and smiled. Standing like that, fingers en-
meshed, with a blueberry sky up above, we watched the
clowns, the marching bands from other towns, and the
floats that were like gigantic cakes. My heart was fat with
love.

Then Mom said, "Here she comes." She stood on tip-
toe, craning her neck to get a better view of the float still
two blocks away. She virtually ignored Droopy the clown,
who was right in front of us, walking on his white-gloved
hands. I watched him, though; watched his sweet sad
face and the black-painted tear until he was out of sight.
The next float carried Miss Coast Guard USA.

Her name was Lisa. I knew because Mom had
pointed out her picture in the newspaper to me. Mom
said that she had just graduated from Grand Haven High
School. Now she was elevated on a platform decorated
with tissue paper rosettes. She was wearing a crown like
the one Mom wore in the family album. Her dark hair
was piled upon her head. Three other young women
were arranged at her feet like handmaidens. All four of
them waved at the spectators lined along the sides of the
road. I waved back. I felt Mom's grip loosening on my
other hand. For a moment, I was worried that she would
break away from me and hitch a ride aboard, leaving us
behind.

"Mom," I said, pulling at her arm. "When do I get to
open my presents?"

The float carrying the Coast Guard Queen signalled
the end of the parade. People were beginning to fold up
their lawn chairs. Mom focused upon me and smiled
slightly. "Later, Elise. You have to wait a bit."

Back home, Dad let us run through the sprinkler
while he watered the lawn. I figured Mom was in the
house getting everything ready for my birthday party.
She would lay out special napkins printed with flowers

and cone-shaped party hats. She'd tack crepe paper to the walls and sprinkle glitter on the tablecloth. I expected to see the proof of her preparations when I went inside to change into dry clothes, but I stood there dripping onto the kitchen linoleum, and saw that everything was the same as usual. The plastic placemats had not been replaced with white damask. Nothing suggested that a celebration was about to take place. And where was Mom? She hadn't come rushing with a bath towel to sop up the puddle I was making.

I grabbed a dish towel from the refrigerator handle and mopped up the water myself. I peeled off my bathing suit and tossed it into the sink. Then I scurried naked down the hall to my room. I was digging around in a drawer in search of clean underwear when I heard a whimper from the room next door. Still naked, I tiptoed out of my room and put my ear against the closed door of my parents' room. I could just barely make out Mom's sniffles. I pushed the door open as quietly as I could, but the hinges creaked anyhow.

Mom looked up and saw me. She was sitting on the edge of her bed, bent over from a sorrow that seemed to start in her stomach. Odder than the sight of her tears was the dress that she was wearing. The blue tulle of the skirt puffed out around her so that it looked like she was floating on a cloud. Satin hugged her breasts.

Mom sat up straight and opened her arms to me. I flew into her embrace. Over her pearly, powdered shoulder, I saw that the zipper was only done up halfway. Little hills of flesh pressed against the fabric.

"It doesn't fit anymore, baby," she said, rocking me gently. "It doesn't fit."

"Ask Daddy to buy you a new dress," I said.

But she didn't like my idea. It only made her cry harder.

3

The kids in our neighborhood usually avoided Mrs. Churchill's house on Halloween night because she handed out religious comics instead of candy. The whole point of Halloween, after all, was Snickers bars and red licorice and lollipops with chocolate centers. It wasn't worth the trek up that long, steep driveway for something that you could get at Sunday school.

Mrs. Churchill was, however, on our trick-or-treat circuit. We had to go there because Dad always went with us, and he couldn't stand the thought of Mrs. Churchill sitting alone with her pamphlets, waiting for children who never came.

I'd been up this driveway many times before, wearing my green fish-tailed skirts and seashell necklaces. I'd even been inside the house. In the days before the neighborhood mothers became working women, there was a weekly coffee klatch. Mom always referred to it as simply "coffee." Coffee was held at a different house every week, and so Mrs. Churchill's turn came up in the rotation from time to time. Before we started school, Amanda and I always went along with Mom. We ate sugar cookies and drank fruit punch while the mothers rehashed their favorite soap operas and traded hints for removing crayon marks from wallpaper.

While most of the living rooms of my childhood had become a blur, I remembered Mrs. Churchill's for its air of formality. The mothers spoke more softly in that living room, their speech metered by the tick of a grandfather clock. When we went to Mrs. Churchill's, and only then, we wore white gloves and patent leather shoes.

On this afternoon, I was dressed in my usual summer attire—denim shorts and a polo shirt. Mom hadn't mentioned a dress code. I carried a loaf of banana bread that Mom had made for me to take.

Mrs. Churchill's house seemed too big for just one person. Most of the houses in the neighborhood had only one story, but hers had two. The second had dormer windows like lidded eyes. The lawn was green and shorn, spongy beneath my feet. I wondered what neighborhood boy was called upon to mow it.

Once, when we were in a money-making mood, Amanda and I had trudged up the hill to offer our services. We'd said we'd keep her grass short for five dollars a week. Mrs. Churchill had looked down with faint disdain. "Dear girls," she'd said, "lawn care is a man's job. You should consider babysitting."

I was breathing hard by the time I reached the brick steps to the porch. I rang the doorbell and the door opened almost immediately.

"Good afternoon, Mrs. Churchill." Ever since we'd read *Great Expectations* at school, I'd pictured her in Miss Havisham's wedding gown so I was surprised to see her wearing a burgundy knit turtleneck dress. Her blue-gray hair was salon-styled, swirled and lacquered. Her lipstick was of a deep dark hue to match her dress. The glasses on a chain around her neck were as I had remembered them.

"Good afternoon, Elise. Won't you come in?" She held the storm door open as I stepped inside.

I was careful to wipe my feet on the mat first. I handed her the bread. "My mother made it."

Mrs. Churchill nodded. "Your mother is a fine woman." She left me for a moment to put the bread in the kitchen, then returned, gesturing grandly. "Come, come. Chiara is waiting for us in the parlor. She's been looking forward to meeting you."

"Likewise, I'm sure," I muttered.

"What was that, dear?"

"Oh, nothing important, Mrs. Churchill." I followed her to the room that most people I knew referred to as the living room. My eyes trailed over the tasteful porcelain figurines. I remembered the framed still life in the hallway. The runner carpet hushed my footsteps.

In the parlor there was a modest chandelier and a shelf of over-sized books with artists' names on their spines—Matisse, Cezanne, Van Gogh. A linen-draped table at the center of the room was set up with a teapot and dainty cups on matching saucers. I took note of the cookies and the silver sugar tongs, then looked up to find a red-headed gamine in printed gauze and heavy bangles enthroned upon a velvet-upholstered chair.

As I entered the room, the young woman smiled brightly and sprang up to meet me. When she came closer, I saw that her eyes were two different colors—one was gray, the other blue.

"Elise, I'd like you to meet my granddaughter, Chiara," Mrs. Churchill said. "She'll be staying with me for these next few months."

"Hello," I said. "Nice to meet you."

"Howdy." Chiara's voice came out soft and warm.

We shook hands under Mrs. Churchill's watchful eyes. She nodded in approval then took a step back. "I'll leave you two young ladies to get acquainted."

I sat down in the opposite chair and kicked off my

Topsiders. I never wanted to wear those shoes again, I thought, staring at Chiara's perfect black boots. I realized the shoes I'd been so proud to own only a few weeks before had nothing to do with the person I wanted to become. I thought about the flowered dresses, the wool crewnecks, and the plaid skirts in my closet and wanted to throw them into the Grand River. I had a sense that my new life was about to begin and I needed a new wardrobe to go with it.

Chiara poured us each a cup of tea. Then she reached into her skirt pocket and pulled out a pack of cigarettes. "Want one?"

"No, thanks." I'd never smoked a cigarette before and I was quite sure that I didn't want my first experience to be in Mrs. Churchill's parlor. I could only imagine what my mother would say.

"Doesn't your grandmother mind?" I asked as she put a cigarette between her reddened lips and lit it. She inhaled deeply before answering.

"Don't worry about Grammy. She's too polite to make a scene in front of guests."

I stole a worried glance toward the doorway. When I heard footsteps clicking overhead, I relaxed a little.

"So where are you from?" I asked, just to get a conversation going.

She laughed lightly. "Oh, just about everywhere. It depends on whom Mother's married to at the moment. We've been living in Memphis, but before that it was France."

I felt a twinge of envy. Here, before me, was a seasoned world traveler, and I'd never even left the Midwest. Chiara must have dozens of interesting stories to tell, I thought. I hoped I'd get to hear as many of them as possible.

"How long are you here for?" I suddenly hoped she'd

stay forever.

"God knows." Chiara rolled her eyes toward the ceiling, waving her cigarette around as she spoke. Her bracelets jangled. "Until Mother gets her life together. She's getting divorced. Again. I guess I'll be here 'til she gets Charles out of her hair. She can't deal with more than one thing at a time, so she sent me here. Mother figures that Grammy will keep me out of trouble."

She smiled then, and I knew her mother was wrong. I hoped she'd drag me into some of that trouble with her.

"I went to boarding school for a while, but I hated it. Those uniforms, lights out at ten, the headmistress from hell...ugh! My father said that I didn't have to go back this year. He's into democracy and all that. He was a hippy before he went establishment. Now he wants me to have a normal life like a normal kid, at least until I come into my trust fund."

"Why don't you live with your father?"

Chiara wrinkled her nose. "I don't live with my father because I abhor my stepmother. I wouldn't live with her if you held a gun to my head."

"That bad, huh?"

Chiara shrugged. "She's stupid and she's too young for my father. Classic case. So what about your parents? I hear your mother was Miss Coast Guard."

I blushed. "It's embarrassing." Mom's beauty queen crown was the last thing I wanted to talk about, and I didn't think Chiara would be too interested in Dad's farmboy upbringing or his basketball scholarship. Compared to Chiara's hippy father and much-married mother, my family was as dull as dirt.

"My great-grandmother was a wreck diver," I said.

Chiara took a drag. "Cool. Tell me more."

Honestly, most of what I knew about her, I'd picked up from library books and yellowing newspaper clippings. "Well," I began, "she mostly helped to recover things like lumber and copper, but one time a rich man asked her to go deep down into a sunken barge and bring back a diamond ring. The guy had left it in his cabin."

Chiara leaned closer. "Go on."

"Back then they didn't have scuba suits. She was decked out in this huge helmet with twenty pounds of lead attached to her feet."

Chiara chimed in with something about the mafia.

"The air went into her helmet through a long tube that was hooked up to a compressor on deck. Then at one point suddenly her oxygen got cut off. Someone had actually tripped over the air compressor and the tube disconnected."

The ash on Chiara's cigarette had grown long. It was about to drop off onto her lap. "And then what happened?" she asked.

I nodded to her cigarette and waited for her to tap off the ash. "Well, she tugged on the rope to let them know up top that she was in trouble."

"Did she give up?"

"No, when she could breathe again, she went and got the diamond ring. The man gave her a reward, and it was in the newspaper." I didn't tell her about the mermaid. Not then. The story was already almost too incredible to be believed.

"Wow! You've got a bona fide heroine in your family history."

I allowed myself a moment of pride before telling Chiara the rest. "We don't talk about her much. Her life was a scandal. She left her husband and kids and ran off with a guy half her age."

Chiara nodded. "Love is a crazy thing."

4

About a month after I had seen Chiara for the first time, a month after I had found Mom crying in her Miss Coast Guard dress, I started kindergarten. Every morning I jumped out of bed, went to the bathroom, and then to the kitchen where Mom was making breakfast. During the day I played Duck Duck Goose and Red Rover and sang songs. At noon I rode the bus home, sometimes with a picture I'd crayoned, which Mom would post on the refrigerator. At dinner, Dad would ask me what I'd learned that day and I'd tell him all about the guinea pig we were keeping in the classroom and how I'd escaped being "it" during tag.

One evening, after I'd finished describing the sights and sounds of the nature walk that morning, Mom said, "Maybe I should get a job. The kids are getting big and they won't be needing me so much anymore." She paused to cut Amanda's pot roast into bite-sized pieces, then without looking up said, "Mamie Williams has started nursing school."

Dad buttered his bread in silence. She looked at him for a long time, then sighed. "Here. Have some more potatoes."

Maybe Dad was worried that if Mom went to work, she'd get her hair frosted like Mrs. Williams or she'd start laying out in a bikini on sunny weekends listening to rock 'n' roll and drinking beer. Sometimes when Amanda and I looked through the slats in the fence dividing our property, we could see Mrs. Williams lying face down on a blanket with her bikini top untied. We never saw Mr. Williams—not even on Saturdays when the other men in the neighborhood were out mowing their lawns.

Mom didn't say any more about going to work. She got up early every morning and made our breakfasts as usual, bustled around with her feather duster in the afternoons, patched our scraped knees with bandages, and stirred up pitchers of fruit punch. As usual. Until one morning, just before Thanksgiving, when not Mom, but Dad came into my room to wake me up.

Actually, I was already awake, mulling over the day's contribution to show-and-tell. I'd already brought in the abandoned bird's nest that I'd found in the juniper tree at the corner of our yard. Another time I'd shown a picture of Mom in her Miss Coast Guard regalia, and once I'd brought in a giant mollusk sent by Grandma and Grandpa from Florida. But on this November morning, I was stumped. Unless I made up a story, something that I'd done in desperation before, I would have nothing to share. So there I was, flat on my back, racing through my brain like a mouse through a maze when Dad switched on the light.

"Daddy," I said, startled. Then I whispered, "Don't turn on the light. You'll wake up Amanda."

"Oh." He flicked the switch again. "Rise and shine, sleepyhead. Breakfast is on the table."

The curious break in routine made me forget, for a moment, my dilemma.

At my place at the table, there was a bowl of cornflakes doused in milk. The cereal had already gone soggy, and the flakes fell apart in my mouth like wet cardboard.

"Daddy, where's my toast with butter and jam?" I asked. "And where's Mom?"

"One piece of toast coming right up!"

I watched him flit from counter to toaster to refrigerator. He was humming.

After he had pressed the toaster lever down, he sat across from me and looked at me very closely as if he were trying to memorize every freckle. "Mom isn't feeling well. It seems there's a little baby doing somersaults in her tummy."

My mind went blank for a minute. Then it came to me. "You mean Mommy's pregnant?"

Dad smiled so that all his teeth showed, even the silver one at the side of his mouth. "That's exactly right, Elise. In a few months, you and Amanda will have your very own baby brother or sister. What do you think of that?"

Suddenly I was awash with relief. Dad had given me a topic for show-and-tell. Now I wouldn't have to make up a story. "I'm very happy, Daddy," I said, "But next time please don't put milk on my cereal until I sit down."

At noon when the yellow bus dropped me off, I was surprised to see a big, long truck in the Williams's driveway. Chairs, end tables, and a black vinyl couch were sitting on the lawn. Men in matching gray coveralls carried huge boxes and fed them into the open mouth of the truck. Mrs. Williams stood under the carport. She looked lonely standing still by herself while the men moved past her, busy as ants. Her frosted hair was hidden under a scarf, and her eyes were masked by dark glasses. A cigarette smoldered between her fingers. From time to time, she blew puffs of smoke into the air. I waved at her, but she didn't wave back. She might have been looking in another direction. It was hard to tell with those glasses.

I found Mom in bed. She was still wearing her night-gown and her face was sickly pale. Amanda sat on the floor beside her with a pile of picture books, pretending to read.

"Hi, sweetie," Mom said in a flat voice. She reached out an arm to me, and I went over and kissed her. She smelled different—a little stale, like clothes worn too long.

"Why is the Williams's furniture outside?" I asked.

"They're moving. Mr. and Mrs. Williams are getting a divorce."

I knew a little about divorce. Brad McCarthy's parents were divorced. He was in my kindergarten class, and during show-and-tell he often displayed the toys that his father bought him on the weekends. They were always marvelous—a battery-powered car, a kite shaped like an airplane, a talking G.I. Joe doll with a scuba suit. His father took him to the circus in Muskegon, and once all the way to Ohio to an amusement park, which Brad said was like the Coast Guard carnival, only better. He didn't talk about his mother very much, although he lived with her during the week.

"Why are the Williamses getting a divorce?"

Mom sighed. "I don't know, honey."

I could tell she was tired of my questions, so I decided to be quiet for a while.

Mom hoisted herself out of bed. She moved slowly, like Grandma when her arthritis was acting up. "Come on, girls," she said. "I'll fix you a peanut butter and jelly sandwich."

After lunch, Mom took a nap. Amanda and I climbed the fence that ran along our property and watched the commotion next door. It was like seeing a body turned inside out. All the things that had been kept private inside the walls of the house were now in plain view for everyone to see. I wondered what the house was like inside, emptied and hollow. And who would live there next?

There was no trace of Mrs. Williams or the furniture the next afternoon. Someone had stabbed a "for sale" sign into the front yard. The grass had already grown shaggy, making it look as if no one had lived there for a long time.

I found Mom jumping rope on the back patio. The weather was cool and breezy, but her forehead was shiny with sweat. I watched the rope loop round and round her body.

"Mommy," I said.

The rope went slack and fell from her hands. Her fingers fluttered to her heart. "Elise! You're home already! I guess I lost track of the time."

I studied her face, trying to find some clue to her odd behavior.

"Listen, honey," she said. "Don't tell Daddy about this, okay?" She gestured toward the rope coiled on the ground.

"Why not?" I asked.

She put her hands on my shoulders and bent down so we were the same height. "It'll be our little secret. Now promise me you won't tell."

I was confused, but I wanted her to be happy. I drew a cross over my heart. "I promise."

"That's my girl." Mom pulled me against her and hugged me tightly. By the time Dad came home, she was back in her nightgown, curled up under blankets.

5

Mom was waiting for me at the door when I got home from tea.

"How'd it go?" Her fingers were knotted, her knuckles white.

"Fine," I said. I made to move past her, but she laid a hand on my arm.

"Mrs. Churchill tells me that there have been some problems in that family and that Chiara might be a little, well, disturbed."

My back stiffened.

"Mrs. Churchill hopes that you'll be a good influence on her granddaughter."

What did she think I was? A social worker? Besides, there was nothing wrong with Chiara that I could see.

"I think Chiara and I hit it off," was all I said.

Mom's fingers slid apart. "Good," she said. "I'm glad. I've already invited her over for dinner tomorrow night. I thought it'd be nice for her to be in a family environment."

She talked as if Chiara was an orphan, but I knew that she'd spent time in just about every sort of family imaginable—the nuclear family with both parents present, the one-parent family, the makeshift family with fake siblings at boarding school, and the step-family.

Ours was just another variation on a theme.

Chiara arrived on our doorstep wearing a billowy white peasant blouse and a skirt spangled with tiny mirrors. Appliqued elephants paraded across the hem. Her fingers were wrapped around a bouquet of daisies. They were loose, not ribboned or wrapped in cellophane.

"I picked them myself," Chiara said, handing them to my mother. She beamed like a cherub.

"Oh!" Mom gathered the flowers into her hands. A ladybug crept out of the stems and onto her wrist. She ignored it and said, "I'll just put these in some water. Make yourself at home, dear."

While Mom was hunting up her cut-crystal vase, I escorted Chiara into the living room to meet my father.

Normally when we had company, Mom went all out, digging up complicated recipes from one of her thick cookbooks written by Jacques something-or-other. She spent hours in the kitchen and it showed. Her repertoire included everything from coq au vin to bird's nest soup. The menu that night, however, was meat loaf, mashed potatoes and gravy, green peas, and blueberry muffins. It was the kind of food that you could order in any cheap diner in America, almost a parody of good home cooking.

We sat down to eat—Mom and Dad at either end, Chiara on my left, Amanda opposite me. The vase of daisies had been placed at the center of the table. The ladybug was nowhere in sight.

Dad said grace, and the rotation of platters and bowls began. Mom kept an eye on Chiara, ready to register the slightest sign of pleasure.

"Oh! Peas!" Chiara's eyes widened.

I couldn't tell at first if she was mocking the dinner or if she was genuinely thrilled. Amanda raised her eyebrows. My sister was not given to raptures about food.

Since she'd entered high school, she saw it as something that could only make you fat. Peas, for example, were higher in calories than most any other vegetables.

We all watched as Chiara scooped a huge mound of peas onto her plate. She passed the dish on to my father, her bangles ringing together. When all plates had been filled and we'd begun chewing away, Chiara picked up one round little pea with her thumb and forefinger. She held it for a moment like a jewel before popping it into her mouth.

Mom saw this. She saw everything. I could sense the great will she summoned to maintain her hostessy exterior. Her smile wilted into a bewildered frown, and she cast her eyes aside. I swear, I could read her mind. *Chiara is, well, a bit disturbed. We have to overlook her quirks and make her feel welcome. It's not her fault she doesn't know how to use silverware.*

Chiara ate all of her peas with her fingers, and no one said a word. Then she took up her knife and fork and ate the meat loaf with impeccable form.

I tried hard not to laugh.

I helped Mom clear the plates away before dessert. She'd made strawberry shortcake, one of her house specialties.

"Do you think she'll know how to eat this?" Mom whispered.

"Of course. She's from earth, you know."

"There's no need to be fresh," she hissed. She brushed past me with the dessert plates.

Amanda, as usual, refused dessert as if it were toxic. Chiara, on the other hand, devoured two servings with a spoon, to Mom's delight.

"Well, girls, how about a game of cards?" my mother asked when the dishes had been cleared away.

Amanda rolled her eyes toward the ceiling. If Chiara

had been her guest, she would have been dying of embarrassment. Peas and card games? Puh-lease. But this was a show. Mom was staging a Norman Rockwell evening for the troubled, deprived urchin who lived down the lane. So we played hearts and euchre and concentration. Chiara shuffled and dealt with expertise, playing each hand with enthusiasm.

She stayed until almost eleven, when my father drove her home. "Thanks for tonight, Mrs. Faulkner," she said at the door. "I had a ball."

"It was my pleasure," Mom said. "You're a breath of fresh air." I could tell that she meant it.

6

My mother was a woman who baked banana bread and meat loaf for neighbors, who kept the carpets free of lint, and the shelves dusted. She collected pledges for the March of Dimes and attended PTA meetings. But somewhere inside her was the mother whose stomach had gotten bigger and bigger, the woman who hadn't wanted to talk about the new baby growing inside of her. Sometimes that mother had stayed in bed all day, and Dad had brought her trays of soup and ice cream. He'd massaged her feet and back and played with my sister and me in the back yard while she slept.

I remember how winter had melted into spring, and the days turned balmy. Gentle breezes fragrant with lilacs ruffled the grass. The crab apple tree in our front yard was in bloom. At night, Amanda and I slept with the window open. As I lay in bed after a story and prayers, I could hear bugs colliding with the screen. The tight mesh kept the mosquitoes out, but not the tinier no-see-ums. They buzzed maddeningly around my head.

One night, I was fast asleep, drifting between dreams when a no-see-um ventured into my ear. I couldn't tell later if it was this invader or the commotion on the other side of the wall that woke me. First, there was an insistent buzz, like a distant motorcycle engine, then the thud of drawers opening and closing, door hinges squeaking, my mother's higher-than-usual voice. I heard clicks and snaps. Hangers jangling like wind chimes. I knew something was wrong. I lay rigid, torn between fear and curiosity.

A few minutes later, Dad opened the door to our bedroom. I squinted at the sudden brightness. Amanda whimpered in her sleep.

"Get up, pumpkin," Dad whispered. "We have to take Mommy to the hospital."

As he gathered Amanda and her blanket in his arms, I went straight to Mom and Dad's room. The bright red splotches on the carpet stopped me cold. I forgot to breathe. My eyes followed the trail of blood from bed to bathroom. I thought my mother was dying.

She was sprawled across the bed, on top of the rumpled sheets, staring at the ceiling. When she heard me come in, she turned her head and offered a weak smile. I was too scared to go to her. I stood in the doorway for what seemed like an hour.

Dad tucked Amanda into the back seat of the station wagon, then came back for Mom and her suitcase. I got into the car without being told.

The streets were bare. Everyone else was sleeping. Dad pushed on the gas pedal as we approached a stop sign. Mom didn't say anything. At the hospital, Dad parked behind an ambulance.

"You girls stay in the car for a minute," he said. "Lock the doors. I'll come back for you as soon as I can."

Mom moaned softly as Dad helped her out of the car. Then a nurse appeared, the white of her uniform luminous in the black night. She was pushing a wheelchair. I felt a burning at the back of my throat and a bitter taste filled my mouth.

"The eensy weensy spider went up the water spout..."

I began to sing softly, trying to calm myself. Hours, days, weeks seemed to go by as I stared at the entrance that had devoured my parents. Big red letters glowed above the glass doors. I couldn't read the word, though I recognized the first letter, E, as in Elise.

I concentrated on each illuminated letter, matching them with the pictures on the kindergarten wall. "M is for mushroom, E is for elephant..." And then I must have fallen asleep because the next thing I knew, I was in a brightly lit room that smelled like medicine, stretched out along a vinyl sofa, feet to feet with Amanda. The room was filled with empty chairs. Magazines with torn covers were fanned out on low tables. Dad sat beside me, drinking coffee from a Styrofoam cup. His eyes and nose were red.

"Daddy," I said. "Where are we? Where's Mommy?"

"The hospital waiting room. Mommy's upstairs." He choked. "She lost the baby."

I reached over and patted his arm like Mom did to me when I was sad. "Lost" didn't sound so bad. "Lost" was the mittens I left on the bus which had turned up later in the "found" box at school. "Lost" was the five pounds that Mom became so happy about when she stepped off the bathroom scales.

"What do you mean?" I asked. "Where did she lose it?"

Dad smoothed my hair with the flat of his hand. "Your baby brother died."

After Mom came home from the hospital, Dad continued to make breakfast and, more often than not, dinner as well. She stayed in her bedroom with the curtains drawn, filling the wastebasket with crumpled, tear-soaked tissues.

Dad said Mom had post-partum depression. I heard

SUZANNE KAMATA

him telling Grandma about it on the phone. I didn't know what it meant. I had another theory. I couldn't forget the sight of Mom jumping rope on the patio. Maybe she had hurt the baby with all of that bouncing and now she was feeling sorry, like the way I felt when I accidentally broke one of Amanda's toys.

I did everything I could to cheer her up. I played Old Maid and Candy Land with her and colored pictures for her at school. But she didn't seem happy when she won a game, and she didn't tape my pictures of tulips and butterflies to the refrigerator door as she had before.

"It's all right, Mommy," I told her. "I don't need a brother anyway."

She laughed for a second, but then tears began streaming down her face.

Then one day, Dad came home from work with his suit jacket hooked on one hand and two long folders clutched in the other.

"Do you know what these are, Elise?" He bent down so I could get a closer look. Pictures of clouds and airplanes covered the folders. Dad's eyes were sparkly.

I shook my head.

"They're airplane tickets. I'm going to take Mom on a little vacation to help her feel better."

"Can I go, too?" I'd never been on a vacation before. Sometimes kids brought in souvenirs from the trips they took with their families. Brad McCarthy had gone to Disney World with his father during Easter break. He'd come back with black felt mouse ears.

"Why don't you and Amanda stay here and keep Grandma company? She's coming to visit tomorrow."

My excitement faded away. It wasn't fair for them to leave us behind.

Dad noticed my disappointment. "Just this one time," he said, drawing me into a hug. "We all want Mommy to get better, don't we?"

Mom didn't seem very excited about going on a trip. She didn't whoop or holler or start twirling around like I thought she would, but she did get out of bed. That evening after supper (Dad made hotdogs), I found her in her nightgown, packing a suitcase. She moved like a zombie, folding cotton blouses and madras sundresses in slow motion. I watched as she tucked sandals into shoe bags and dropped her bathing suit onto piles of clean underwear. I wanted to ask her many questions, but they jammed in my throat. I could tell she was tired. I could tell she was sick.

"You be good for Grandma, you hear?"

"Yes, Mom. I promise with all of my heart."

Before we went to bed, Dad called Amanda and me into the living room. He was holding the M volume of the World Book encyclopedia. "Come here, my little sugarplums. I'll show you where we're going."

My sister and I scrambled onto his lap and studied the pictures as Dad explained. They were going to a place called Acapulco. Dad said that it was in another country—not the U.S.A., but Mexico. "They speak a different language there," he said.

I remembered. Mom had told us about Mexico before, in the story of how she'd become Miss Coast Guard. "I could speak Spanish," she'd explained, "and I could tap dance, so I told the judge that I wanted to go to poor countries like Mexico and Bolivia and dance for the people. I would bring smiles to their faces and make their lives a little less hard to bear."

"They speak Spanish," I said now. I wondered if Mom would tap dance in Acapulco.

Dad laughed. "Yes, that's exactly right. What a clever girl you are."

"Spanish!" Amanda shouted. Even then, she couldn't

stand to be outdone. "Span! Ish! Span! Ish!"

It took a minute for Dad to calm her down.

I was fascinated by the pictures. In Mexico, men wore big straw hats to hide from the sun and took naps called siestas. In Mexico, there were poinsettias and piñatas filled with candy.

"I'll bring you back a souvenir," Dad said. "What do you want?"

"Candy!" Amanda shouted.

"Jumping beans. And a Mexican doll."

Their homecoming would be like a holiday. We'd get presents and Mom would be happy again.

Grandma arrived with her two matching green suitcases and her hatbox. Grandpa stayed behind at their bungalow in Florida. He didn't come because he was afraid of flying. In the war, his plane had almost gone down behind enemy lines, and he'd lost his taste for air travel. "And besides," Grandma said, "he doesn't like airplane food."

She installed herself in Mom and Dad's room since we didn't have a guest room. Mom had stripped the bed and put out clean sheets for Grandma. By the time I came home from school that day, she'd hung her clothes in the closet and arranged her shower cap and toothbrush in the bathroom. The house smelled different with Grandma there. She trailed the scent of rose water and fabric softener.

In kindergarten we were learning how to tell time. We had all made clocks out of boxes, cartons, odds and ends. Some of the kids had cut pendulums and cuckoos out of cardboard. Mine was basic—a square box with a white paper face pasted on. At school, Mrs. Howard would say, "It's nine o'clock" or "ten fifteen," and we would adjust the hands on our handmade clocks so they told the correct time. At home, I tired to impress Grandma by announcing the time every chance I got.

"Grandma, guess what? It's three o'clock. Time for snacks."

She chopped up apples for Amanda and me. We crunched on them dutifully, wondering what she'd done with the windmill cookies Mom usually gave us.

"Grandma, ask me what time it is now," I said, after I'd brushed my teeth.

She sighed. "All right. What time is it?"

"It's three twenty-five."

After a while, she seemed to go deaf. She stopped looking at the wall clock to check my accuracy. That is, until I announced that it was time for "I Dream of Jeannie."

"How about if we don't watch any television programs tonight?" she asked.

I couldn't believe it. How could she be so mean? Mom always let us watch the show about the genie who lived in a bottle. Sometimes she even watched with us.

"You may not believe this," Grandma said, "but too much TV rots the brain. Why don't we play a game together instead? Or read a book?"

I didn't think playing a game was such a good idea. If Amanda lost, she'd start bawling, and then we'd be in for a big lecture about cry babies and being good sports. "Let's look at the family album," I said.

"All right."

I told Grandma where to sit and heaved the album onto her lap. Amanda and I took our places beside her. I reached over and turned to the first page. There was a black and white picture of a young man in a sailor uniform. He had a dimple in his chin, like Dudley Do-Right on "Bullwinkle," and he was holding a baby—my mother.

"This is my brother," Grandma said softly. "You

never met your Great Uncle Joe, but I can tell you he was a nice man."

"What happened to him?" I asked, although I already knew.

"He was in the Coast Guard during the war. He was on the Escanaba when it was bombed. The ship sank and only two men survived."

"Why didn't Great Grandma rescue him?" I asked. I'd already heard a few things about my mother's grandmother, and how she dove into deep water, bringing up treasures. To me, she was a super hero in a swimsuit.

Grandma snorted and turned the page. "She wasn't that kind of woman."

Next, there was a photo of Grandma and Grandpa before her hair turned white and Grandpa's fell out and their middles went soft. Grandma was very beautiful, I thought, but in a different way from Mom. Her hair was dark and permed and her eyes a velvety brown. In the picture, Mom, at about two years old, toddled between her parents.

"Julia was such a fussy baby," Grandma said, shaking her head. "I had such a terrible time putting your mother down to take a nap, and she was always getting into things—the cupboards, my purse, the wastebaskets."

I squirmed. This was different from looking at the album with Mom. She made the stories of the past seem like fairytales, but Grandma's memory was a repository of hard times and annoyances. She told us about the winter it snowed so hard that cars were buried and the road went unplowed for a week. "We ran out of milk and I couldn't get to the store to buy more. I think that's why your mother ended up with so many cavities," she said.

I flipped to the page where Mom sat on a piano stool. Maybe Grandma would tell us about the pretty dresses with lace and ruffles and crinolines that Mom wore for her recitals, I thought. I wanted to hear her hum a few bars of "Fur Elise" like Mom did when we got to this part. She always told me that I was the only one in the family with my own special song.

Grandma tapped her finger on the picture and clucked her tongue. "Your mother was always a flighty one."

I pictured Mom in plumage, angel's wings carrying her over neighborhood houses, her bare feet skimming the tops of the maples and oaks that lined our street. With feathers she would be able to fly over the silky soft dunes and the green-gray waters of Lake Michigan, then moonward, as far as the stars. I marveled over this image for a moment, although I could tell by Grandma's voice that she meant something else. What if Mom one day flew away from us forever? What if she never came back from Mexico?

Grandma was still talking. I tuned in to her rambling. "First," she said, "Julia wanted to study ballet, and then she wanted to ride horses. She had no sense of commitment. Not even to her studies or that boyfriend she had. What was his name? Ted? He was such a lovely young man. Wonderful manners! He's a doctor now, I hear. In Kalamazoo. Ahh, well. That's all water under the bridge. Maybe your father will talk some sense into her down in Mexico and she'll start taking some responsibility for her actions."

I didn't want to look at the pictures any more. I guessed that Grandma didn't either. She kept changing the subject, fast-forwarding then sliding into the past. Her words had nothing to do with the pictures. Amanda was slumped against Grandma's shoulder and her eyes were closed. A thin string of drool hung from her cracked-open mouth.

"Grandma, can I please, please watch the end of 'I

Dream of Jeannie'?" I could tell by the clock that there were just ten minutes left—enough time to see the happily-ever-after ending.

She sighed deeply, her heavy bosom riding like shifting mountains. "Oh, all right. And then it's time for bed." She shut the album with a thump.

Grandma stayed with us for a week. My parents' absence was complete—there were no phone calls or letters, and the post card Mom sent didn't arrive until after my parents had returned.

They stepped off the plane in summer clothes, though June in Michigan was still a little chilly, their skin a shade or two darker than before. Dad was wearing one of those big hats I'd seen in the encyclopedia. Colorful little pompoms dangled from the brim. Mom had a brand new straw tote bag slung over one shoulder. In her hands were two brightly painted rattles that looked like darning eggs. "Maracas," she told me later. They must have looked like dawn stragglers from some costume party to Grandma in her linen suit and sensible shoes.

Grandma pursed her lips at the sight of them rumba-ing across the tarmac. Amanda and I, however, were delighted. Our darling, dancing mother was back. Our lives would go on as before.

But they didn't. In spite of the forced gaiety which sustained us through the first few days of Mom and Dad's return, things had changed. I wasn't sure what had happened down there, what they had done in Mexico besides beachcombing and star-gazing and haggling at the markets, but something had.

Mom did not go back to bed. She was filled with energy and spent it cleaning the house with grim determination. Whenever I saw her, she was armed with a feather duster or a bleach bottle. And she had forsaken the pink rubber gloves that had shielded her soft hands and painted nails before. Now, when she touched me, her hand on my cheek was rough.

One afternoon, eager for a chat, I was lucky to find Mom in the living room. She was resting on the sofa, having a cup of coffee between mopping the kitchen floor and ironing.

"Mommy," I began. "Did you speak Spanish in Mexico?"

She laughed shortly. "No, honey. I don't remember a lick of it. Daddy did all the talking when we were down there."

I can't explain why, but this news made me feel sad. I somehow knew that her old stories would be different. They would be dimmer, like faded stars.

When the Coast Guard Festival rolled around again, Mom didn't go with us to the parade. Amanda, Dad and I stood at the curb watching the floats go by. I can't even remember what Miss Coast Guard looked like that year.

7

"I'm putting my dollar on Bethany Miller for Coast Guard queen," Amanda said, one morning not long after our dinner with Chiara. "How about you?"

She was scooping tofu into the blender while I sat at the kitchen table with a bowl of Cocoa Puffs. The newspaper was spread out before me, open to the candidates' photos and bios.

In my ninth grade geometry class, our teacher had held a betting pool for the NCAA basketball championship. I'd won out of sheer luck when the University of Kentucky took the title. Ever since then, I'd been betting with Amanda every chance I got.

My sister always went for the obvious choice—the girl with the blondest, longest hair, with a talent like singing or dancing. In the Miss Coast Guard pageant, at least, I always picked the underdog.

"Jennifer Kowalski," I said. She had kind of a big nose and her smile was crooked. For the talent portion, she was going to read her own poetry. I could tell she hadn't been to charm school and wasn't headed for a modeling career. Her teeth weren't shiny like Bethany's, but I wanted her to win.

Amanda laughed. "You might as well hand your money over right now, sister."

I ignored her and took a gulp of orange juice.

I was still in my pajamas, but Amanda was dressed for the beach. In a little while, the love of my life would come and whisk her away to the State Park for a day of fun in the sun. I saw a movie of them in my mind— Amanda and Clark Henderson, running hand in hand along the edge of the water in slow motion, the sun setting behind them. I gritted my teeth.

For as long as I could remember, I'd wanted Clark for my boyfriend. He held the record for the hundred-yard dash at our school and he was captain of the football team. And although he was tall and funny and gorgeous, he'd deigned to be my lab partner in eighth grade biology. That's as close as I'd ever gotten.

We'd chatted in line at the cafeteria, but never sat together for lunch. And then one day, while I was digging into my brown bag, he came over and dropped down on the seat beside me. He rested his chin in his palm and looked up at me as if I owned the moon. I was sure that everyone around me could hear my heart pounding.

"So tell me, Elise," he said, "is your sister going out with anyone?"

I'd thought about lying, but then I imagined him in our house and on our phone. Maybe if he spent enough time around me, he'd see that I was the one for him. But so far I was wrong. They'd been going out for months now.

"Are you guys going to the carnival tonight?" I asked Amanda.

"Naw. I think we're going to see a movie."

I breathed out a sigh of relief. The night before, I'd made plans to go to the carnival with Chiara. I didn't want to run into Amanda and Clark.

From the time Clark pulled up in his red Camaro, I tried hard not to think about them. I cleaned my room, read, and watched TV. Finally, I called Chiara and told her I was coming over.

"Oh, good," she said. "Grammy's at bridge."

She met me at the door. I trailed after her past the ceramic shepherdess and the bowl of apples, up the stairs, down the hall, and into her bedroom. The walls were plastered with a collage of posters, pictures cut out of magazines, post cards, and photographs. I recognized Billie Holiday in one of the pictures, a gardenia tucked in her hair, her mouth open in song at the mike. I'd read about her and seen pictures of her before, but I'd never heard her music. There were other pictures: an inky black man cradling a saxophone, Marilyn Monroe on the beach hugging herself against the cold, Louise Brooks wearing a long string of pearls that reached to her knees. Chiara had thrown a length of Indian cloth over the bed. On the nightstand she'd arranged an assortment of candles, tiny lacquered boxes, and an incense burner.

"Would you like something to drink?" she asked.

I was thinking Coke or maybe tea, like the other day. "Yes, please." I waited for a china cup nestled in its lilac sprigged saucer, but Chiara reached under her bed and pulled out a half-empty whiskey bottle. She screwed off the top and handed it to me.

I held the bottle uncertainly, looking around for a glass or a mug, maybe some ice. I wasn't up on the etiquette of hard liquor. For all I knew, I needed a brown paper sack. I'd had a few secret sips of beer, but I wasn't a regular at the weekend high school parties. Amanda went to them sometimes, with a carload of friends. When she came back, she told me who the pot smokers were and who had been locked in a bedroom together. When Clark's parents were in Jamaica, there was a three-keg party at his house. Afterwards, Amanda told me who had vomited all over the sofa. I wasn't a part of that crowd, though.

"Go on. Take a swig," Chiara said, noticing my hesitation. "It'll burn at first, but then you'll get this warm, lovely feeling down deep in your stomach." She nodded as I put the bottle to my lips and tilted my head back. I sputtered and coughed, but Chiara didn't laugh.

"Wait a minute," she said. "The good feeling will come." She knelt in front of a stack of records and passed a finger over the titles until she came across what she was looking for. "Chet Baker!" she said. "You gotta hear this!"

I'd never heard of Chet Baker. Most of the kids I knew listened to groups with wild hair and loud twangy guitars: Black Sabbath, Yes, Aerosmith, Van Halen. My own modest record collection was composed of a few old Supremes albums I'd gotten from my mother and some of the requisite heavy metal.

I sat down on the floor, my back against the bed, head already full of fuzz. Chiara, caught up in a quick burst of excitement, was oblivious. I watched as she laid the record on her turntable and set the needle in the groove. Her eyelids closed as a voice as sweet and smooth as syrup filled the room. Eyes still shut tight, her hips began twitching in time with the piano. Her hands moved about in the air as if she were trying to catch the notes of the horn as they flew out into the room.

When the first song had ended, Chiara sat down beside me, her different-colored eyes all aglitter. She was breathless. There was some magic in that music that I hadn't quite grasped, maybe because of the whiskey, maybe because I'd been too busy watching its effect on Chiara to pay much attention. The next time, I would close my eyes, too.

"Well, what do you think?" she asked.

Because I knew it was the answer she was looking for, I said, "I love it."

Chiara nodded, satisfied, unsurprised.

"All right then. Let's go check out that carnival."

Chiara and I entered the carnival grounds, the blinking, flashing, chiming world of temporary fun. I tried to play it cool, flipping my hair back and sighing: another year, another carnival. But Chiara was practically bouncing.

"Look! A merry-go-round!" She was already counting out tickets.

Without exception, the carousel horses were mounted by small children. Some parents stood alongside, spotting them in case of a fall. It was clearly a kiddie ride. What if someone from school saw me there, astride a painted pony?

Chiara didn't seem to notice my reluctance. I tripped along behind her as she dragged me into line.

"The last time I rode one of these was in Avignon," Chiara squealed. "La Place de l'Horloge. It was in the shadow of a castle."

I tried to imagine a palace looming over the carnival. The image was appealing.

When the horses' revolutions slowed and stopped, the little kids in smeared shirts and cartoon-faced sandals got off. They ran in search of balloons and prize animals and cotton candy. Meanwhile, Chiara and I handed over our tickets and hopped onto neighboring horses.

"Whooee! Giddy-up!" Chiara bucked in the saddle and I had to laugh.

A couple of parents exchanged looks and whispered behind their hands. I was starting not to care. I decided that I wouldn't allow myself to feel embarrassed for the rest of the night.

After the merry-go-round, we wandered through the game gallery, through the cries of hawkers, the screams of tiny children, the endless tinkle and chime of carnival rides.

"Wanna see my Annie Oakley impression?" Chiara asked.

"Sure."

She stepped up to a shooting gallery, hoisted a plastic rifle onto her shoulder, and fired off a round of corks. She knocked down three one-dimensional ducks and won a teddy bear.

"What are you going to do with that?" The bear was purple plush, gaudy as could be. Chiara held it in front of her like a dance partner and whirled around a few times. She narrowly missed a young family with a back-strapped baby and a little blond boy.

"Oops," she said. "Sorry." Then she held out the bear to the big-eyed boy. "Here. This is for you."

He hugged it and we were deep into the crowd before the parents had a chance to protest.

"What do you want to do next?" Chiara asked me.

"Umm, how about the Ferris wheel?"

"The Ferris wheel it is!" She went skipping ahead. "You know the last time I was on one of those was in Bordeaux," she called over her shoulder.

I rolled my eyes and tried to catch up with her.

The line snaked around the front of the ride. I threw my head back and looked at the gondolas dangling up above. I hoped that Chiara wouldn't try to make our chair swing while we were mid-air.

"What a dish!" Chiara said, bringing my attention back to the ground.

"What?"

"Look at the guy operating the ride. He is gorgeous!"

I'd never really given much thought to the carnies before. They'd always struck me as rough and a little scary. I'd always assumed that they were uneducated, unpolished. Bums, more or less. Plus, they were only here for a short time and they were too old to be considered boyfriend material. But I looked.

The man at the lever was dark. His black hair was gathered into a ponytail and a red bandana circled his head. The sleeves of his T-shirt had been chopped off and I could see the thick black hair under his arms, the contours of his muscles. The lights from the Ferris wheel danced on his bare arms. He pulled back the bar of each gondola as it came to rest, even steadied a young woman by the elbow when she stumbled on the platform, but he didn't look anyone in the eye. I could tell his thoughts were elsewhere—on the next town, maybe, or whatever he had planned for after work.

I kept watching him, trying to figure out what had attracted Chiara. There had to be something beyond his brooding, his compact body and grace. It's true that the more I studied him, the more alluring he became, but I wasn't sure why. While Chiara stood beside me slapping out a beat on her thighs, I examined his full lips, the lock of hair that fell across his eyes, the pulpy veins rivered across his nut brown arms.

When it was finally our turn, I handed over my ticket. Our fingertips touched and a spark of static electricity jumped between us. He looked up then, into my eyes. I had enough time to take in the golden flecks in his brown irises, the tiny nick of a scar at the corner of his eye, the giraffe lashes.

He didn't say anything, but I felt his eyes upon me the whole time he was buckling us into place. I could feel my body heat up a degree or two. It was as if I'd gulped down a mouthful of fire. Then he yanked on the metal bar to test its security, nodded slightly to us, and turned away.

"He wants you," Chiara said knowingly.

"Don't be ridiculous." I didn't tell her about the shock, but already I was thinking that it was a sign. I spent the entire ride trying to think of something clever to say to him when we got off while Chiara marveled at the view of the Grand River.

"Look at all those boats out there. Do you think they're having a party?"

I didn't bother to look in the direction of her pointing finger. I was watching the action below. Another young man had stepped up to the controls of the Ferris wheel. He and my guy spoke for a moment, and then traded places. I tried to track him through the throng, but he disappeared and I was bereft for the rest of the night.

Ô

The morning after my last day of the fourth grade, Mom, Amanda, and I climbed into the car. The warm vinyl seats sucked the back of our legs. We were all dressed in new bathing suits. Even Mom had bought a new one that year—a bright blue one-piece of a puckered material—to go with her new body, she said. She'd been doing exercises at 6 a.m. with a chair and Jack LaLanne on the television. She'd stopped making cookies. I missed the smell of butter and vanilla warming together and the taste of melted chocolate, but whenever Mom saw me lingering in the grocery store near the cookies, she'd say, "Elise, I think it's about time you lost that baby fat."

If Dad heard Mom, he'd say, "After a summer of playing in the water and running around the beach, she'll be as slender as a twig."

And so, there we were, buckled against the sticky vinyl, our arms shiny with the first application of coconut oil, with sunglasses perched on our noses. According to the weather report on the radio, Lake Michigan was only sixty-five degrees, but a green flag was flying at the Coast Guard station, indicating calm waters. If a yellow or red flag had signaled a strong undertow and surfer waves, we'd be confined to the sandy expanse of beach, the swings and seesaw, or the picnic pavilion. To me, there was no point in going to the beach if you couldn't go in the water.

Mom turned the radio up high as she sometimes did when she was feeling young and happy, and we set off on the mile drive to the shore. Although the park was nearby, we hadn't been there since winter when Dad had taken us to hike over the icebergs.

"At the top of the world, it's like this all over," he said as we climbed the huge crystals.

I remembered the story about my great uncle, on a ship made to cut through the ice. He and the rest of the crew had plowed through these very waters, and also to Greenland and Iceland. They'd rescued more than 150 men from the icy sea at the top of the world after their ships were torpedoed. My uncle's cutter, the Escanaba had been on its way to Newfoundland, another cold place, when it had sunk. I didn't think I could live in a place where wind blew night and day, where it was always too cold to swim. Water was my medium.

Now, Mom parked the car in the sandy lot and we eagerly emerged. The smell of fish was strong, stronger than I remembered from years before. We loaded our arms with towels, a Frisbee, a mini-cooler filled with pop and sandwiches, and Mom's portable radio. All three of us wore brand new flip-flops, although they would gather sand as we dashed down the hill.

Behind the parking lot, a great dune rose like a mountain. Sometimes we climbed it to watch the sun set over the lake. In winter, we flew down its face on a toboggan or saucer.

Amanda, who was only carrying a towel, ran ahead of Mom and me, down the nearly deserted beach. Her feet kicked up clouds of sand as she raced to the edge of the lake. I wanted to join her, but the weight of the cooler was like an anchor holding me back. Almost as soon as she reached the lake, she turned around and began running back to us. Maybe the water was too cold, I thought. I was familiar with the toe-numbing chill of the lake in early summer. But then, as I drew closer, I saw that fish—hundreds of them—were piled along the shoreline. They were floating in the shallows, too, wide-eyed and putrid. The stink blasted me and I had to break away.

Mom saw it, too. "Oh, dear," she said. "I guess we won't be doing any swimming in the lake this summer. We'll have to find something else for you girls to do."

My heart fell like a stone tossed into the lake.

"Maybe someone will clean up the dead fish," I said. I didn't want to spend my summer at vacation Bible school making crosses out of burnt matchsticks or decoupaging Bible verses onto pieces of driftwood.

Mom shook her head sadly. "The lake must be polluted," she said. "I don't think it's safe."

It was too late to sign up for swimming at the Y.M.C.A. pool, but Mom wasn't about to let us hang around the house all summer, running through the sprinklers and hounding her for popsicles. Since Amanda had started school, she had grown possessive of her "private time."

She began stepping out at random moments, leaving me in charge. "Would you keep an eye on your little sister?" she'd say. "I'm just going next door for a cup of sugar. I'll be back in a flash."

Whether it was a cup of sugar of a pinch of salt or an egg to replace the one that had accidentally fallen to the linoleum, I quickly learned that the errand would always take longer than the five or ten minutes Mom promised. She would inevitably be invited to sit down for coffee and a gab session and she'd be gone for half an hour or more.

I didn't mind. If Amanda was absorbed in mothering her dolls in the play room, I would slip away and seek out the mysteries of the house. I liked to sit at Mom's vanity, open her bottles of cologne, and sniff them one by one. When I closed my eyes, Emeraude brought images of Mom in her red shirtwaist and lipstick, about to set off for some charity meeting. The golden liquid in the Chanel No. 5 bottle made me think of Mom in a silk dress with her hair piled high, writing down a phone number for the babysitter.

I sometimes stared long and hard at the mirror, trying to imagine what I would look like in ten years. By then I'd be old enough to marry. Maybe the soft fat at my jaw would melt away, and my face would acquire elegant angles like Mom's.

I opened her compacts, but I didn't dare powder my nose or brush my cheeks with pink. She might have come home before I had had a chance to wash it off. Instead, I went to the walk-in closet and opened the door.

The dresses Mom wore most often were at the front. When I ran my hands over them, little puffs of perfumed air filled my nose. I allowed myself to be intoxicated for just a moment by those wonderful familiar scents of skin and cologne before pushing through to the seldom worn garments at the back.

These clothes were evidence of Mom's secret self, a version of her that I had heard about, but never met. There was her frothy white wedding gown hanging in its zippered plastic case. I parted the zipper a few inches and reached inside to touch the cool taffeta, now slightly yellowed. Next to the gown, deeper in the closet, a party dress was suspended from a satin-padded hanger. It was black and slippery, decorated with fuchsia blossoms of flocked velvet. The dress had straps like my bathing suit, but its skirt billowed like a black cloud, plumped by a crinoline underneath. There was also a fur piece, which I had never seen Mom wear, and a frilly sheer nightgown of blue nylon.

I didn't know what to make of my mother. Sure, I had seen pictures, but with each passing year the gulf between Mom with her aprons and dishpan hands and the mother with the glamorous past became wider. Why did she keep these clothes if she didn't need them? And when would I be able to fit into them?

I went through her drawers, too. I picked through the sachets and scarves and bras. She kept little boxes containing broaches and rings under her panties. These drawers were for intimate things, special things. I found a photo of Dad buried under a pile of silk stockings. He was wearing his college basketball uniform. On the back, he'd written, "Yours, forever." Beneath that, was a yellowed newspaper clipping:

"Mrs. Margaret Stieg has announced her intention to salvage the cargo of the *New Brunswick*, which sank in Lake Erie in 1859. The diminutive diver made a name for herself by bringing up the valuable iron and copper of the old steamer *Pewabic* which sank in Lake Michigan off Thunder Bay in 1865. She feels confident that she will again succeed where others have failed."

Mrs. Stieg, my great-grandmother, appeared in black and white. I'd been told that her hair was as red as a sunset. She had a beauty mark at the corner of her mouth. In this photo, she was holding a huge diving helmet and she was grinning from ear to ear.

In the back of the same drawer, I found something else—a bus ticket. It was imprinted with the silhouette of a greyhound, the mascot of the bus that stopped downtown, and dated six years before. I counted. I'd been four when the ticket was issued. I had never ridden on a bus with a dog painted on its side and neither had Mom, as far as I knew. She had always been with Amanda and me.

I held the ticket in my hand, careful not to smudge

it. The paper was clean and uncreased. It looked brand new. The name of our city was typed at the center of the ticket and the words "Destination: Terre Haute." I had no idea why Mom would go there.

Greyhound. Grand Haven. June 16, 1974. Terre Haute. I puzzled over the ticket for a long while. I didn't put it back until I heard the door open downstairs and Mom called out, "Yoo hoo! I'm home!"

9

The morning after Chiara and I went to the carnival, I threw open my closet door and realized that I had nothing to wear. The crisp cotton blouses with ruffles and Peter Pan collars, the pleated plaid skirts, and the Shetland sweaters had nothing to do with the kind of person I wanted to be. I called up Chiara and said, "Let's go shopping."

"Great," she said. "I know just the place."

Although she'd only arrived a few days before, she'd already discovered Kiki's Closet, a vintage clothing store that had just opened. I hadn't even been there yet.

Kiki was a woman wearing dangly rhinestone earrings and a long lace dress. She smiled sweetly and said "hello" when we walked into the store, but she didn't hover like the clerks at Steketee's or Gimbel's. She stayed where she was, perched on a stool with a paperback, while Chiara and I explored. We tried on hats in front of the long tarnished mirror, petted the elbow-length kidskin gloves displayed in the open drawer of an antique vanity, and danced over the hardwood floor holding poodle skirts up to our waists. Kiki looked up from her book from time to time and smiled.

Some of the clothes were slightly stained or otherwise damaged—a drop of coffee here, a cigarette burn there—but these flaws gave them character. Caressing the sleeve of a silk bed jacket, I wondered what woman in what bed had worn the delicate garment. There were secrets in each pocket, memories lingering in the pleats of skirts, stories in every seam.

I picked out a fake leopard fur coat, a simple black dress in an elegant moire, and poplin pedal pushers like Mom once wore. I also bought a couple of oversized men's jackets that smelled like mothballs, a beaded sweater, and a sleeveless chemise a la Jackie Kennedy.

"Great," Chiara said, as I modeled a paisley shirt. "You're on your way. Now let's go home and do your hair."

Back at home, I retrieved a pair of scissors from the bathroom closet—the ones Mom had used to trim our bangs when Amanda and I were little. I spread some newspapers on the floor and positioned a chair on top of them. Chiara pinned a towel around my neck and set to work. I stared out at the hedges my father had recently pruned and listened to the snip of scissors. Long blonde locks, light and airy as dandelion fluff, fell onto the newspaper, obscuring President Reagan's face, blotting out headlines.

When the job was done, I turned to the mirror and looked at my new image. The ragged clumps of hair and the surprised look in my eyes made me look like a crazy person. But then I looked closer and saw a young woman who would be willing to smuggle secrets in underground Paris. She wouldn't hesitate to ride broncos bareback or do the tango on a tabletop. It's the new you, I told myself. "Hello," I said. "Nice to meet you."

10

Back when I was a little girl, I didn't know how to talk to Mom about the ticket I'd found in the drawer, so I immediately pushed it to the back of my mind.

At any rate, she soon came up with a plan for our summer.

"I'll bet if I ask Miss Burke very nicely, she'd let you join her junior dance class," she said one afternoon as we lounged in front of the TV.

"Oh, goody!" Amanda said. "When can we start?"

My little sister had already decided that she was going to be a ballerina when she grew up. I'm not sure what inspired her, other than a fondness for twirling around in the yard until she toppled from dizziness and an admiration for the tutu-ed figure that danced when she opened her little jewelry box.

"If I had started dance lessons when I was your age, I might have been able to become a professional," Mom said. "It's never too early."

I'll admit that I was looking forward to the first lesson. I thought that it might be a neat trick to be able to walk on my tippy toes.

Les Belles Danseux studio was in a former elementary school that had been converted into a community center. Down the hall there were macrame classes, and aerobic dance was held in the gymnasium. In Miss Burke's room, there were bars and mirrors attached to the walls and three rows of little girls in leotards lined up on the sanded wooden floor.

"Today we'll simply watch," Mom whispered as we stepped into the room. She cleared cast-off leg warmers from the chairs against the wall and motioned for us to sit. No one seemed to notice us. All eyes were fixed on the woman at the head of the class.

She was thin—thinner than my mother in her Miss Coast Guard picture. When she reached her arms above her head, I could count the ribs raised in relief against her leotard. Her chest was almost as flat as Amanda's, not puffed out with soft flesh like mine. Although her body was like a girl's, I could tell that she wasn't young. Her black bun was threaded with white and a deep crease sliced the bridge of her nose.

"Why isn't she married?" I asked. I hadn't met many single older women, though I had read a book about a Miss Isabelle Bird who traveled around the world by herself.

"She was engaged to be married once," Mom whispered. "It was back before I was her student. But her fiancé was killed in a car accident. I guess she never found anyone she loved better than dancing."

I found this story terribly romantic, but it was hard for me to connect it with the severe woman on the dance floor.

"Miss Burke was quite famous in her day," Mom continued. "She danced the role of Sleeping Beauty when she was with the Kansas City Ballet."

Sure enough, there were framed photographs on the wall of Miss Burke in her glory days. Her youth, her improbable contortions, had been captured and frozen on film. She was dressed in filmy gowns, crowned with rhinestones, her face a mask of longing. There was something vague and distant about the woman in these pictures. She wasn't someone you'd go to for comfort. There was no soft place to rest a troubled head, only hard bones and taut skin.

And Miss Burke in-the-flesh was not so different. I was put off by her brisk manner, and the way she snapped at the girl in the back row for stumbling out of line. "Try not to drag behind, Angelina," she barked. "Backs straight, girls! Heads high!"

It really didn't look like much fun at all. I rummaged through my head, trying to come up with some alternative for whiling away my vacation. Maybe there was still a chance of getting into the baton twirling class. I could march in the parade at the end of the summer. But when I turned to tell Mom my idea, I saw the way her cheeks glowed and her eyes sparkled as they followed the budding ballerinas.

"Oh, I can't wait to see my girls on the stage," she said. "I just know I'll be so proud of you!"

The images of parades and batons and sequined costumes faded like fireworks. I couldn't back out now. Mom would be so disappointed.

I watched the little girls lined up before me and I searched their faces for the tiniest hint of joy. Smiles, it seemed, were against the rules. I noted the crumpled brow of one girl, barely concealed by a fringe of blonde bangs. I saw teeth biting lips in concentration, but no smiles.

In the chair next to mine, Amanda swung her legs back and forth, back and forth. She was humming. She really had no idea. She thought this was going to be fun. I was sure that in ballet class there would be no swinging of legs, no flicking of ponytails, and no humming.

Later, some older girls appeared in the doorway. I

recognized a couple of them from school. I figured they were sixth graders. These girls slouched against the door frame, snapped gum, and flipped their hair back at every opportunity. They had such confidence that I was sure they'd been taking dance lessons for years. A couple of them were just getting breasts, and those little mounds of flesh looked somehow wrong in that room full of waifs.

At the end of the beginner's class, Miss Burke clapped her hands and said, "That's all for today."

This seemed to be a cue. The little girls curtsied in unison, saying, "Merci, Mademoiselle," then broke out of formation. Now there were smiles as they gathered up their leg warmers and tote bags and an hour's worth of pent-up chatter poured out of them. The older girls moved into the studio as if taking possession. Without being told, they began stretching and bending in front of the mirrors.

Miss Burke glided over to us. Her movements were all liquid and smooth as if part of a ballet. Even the way she reached out her arms and embraced my mother seemed choreographed. I watched as Miss Burke kissed the air next to my mother's left ear and then her right ear. I had never seen my mother kiss her friends before, and this way of kissing-but-not-kissing was strange for me.

"Julia, darling!" trilled Miss Burke. "It's been too long! Let me look at you..."

And the dance continued as Mom twirled around, laughing, and Miss Burke stood admiring her former star student.

Finally, when my mother and Miss Burke were finished embracing and cooing, their attention turned to Amanda and me.

I felt Miss Burke's gaze travel from my head to my

toes like a cold finger. She pressed her lips into a tight smile which did not reach her eyes and nodded her head just slightly. Then she turned to Amanda. This time her hand reached forward and flitted for a moment over Amanda's ponytail and her bony shoulder.

"This one would make a nice little Clara," she said to Mom. "We're doing *The Nutcracker* this winter."

Although I was sure that Amanda had no idea what Miss Burke was talking about, my sister knew that she had been singled out. Chosen. She smiled brightly and stood taller than before. I sensed then that, for Miss Burke, she would stop fidgeting and turn out to be some kind of child wonder.

11

In water, I flowed. I floated. I oozed. I moved with fluid grace, at one with the waves. In the dance class that Mom dragged us to once a week that summer, I had too many limbs. They warred with each other, and made me trip and fall. My body turned against me. By late July, I could arrange my feet in first, second, and third position. Even the demi-plies felt easy enough, but when I looked into the mirror I saw that my movements were jerky. Things got worse when Miss Burke set the phonograph needle in the groove of a record and we were supposed to dance. Jazz, tap, ballet—I was bad at all of them.

"Elise, keep that back straight," Miss Burke shouted at least once a class. She herself could have carried books on her head.

One sizzling day, I was in the middle of a demi-plie when a strange pain shot through my abdomen. I bent over in surprise, sure that I had attracted Miss Burke's attention. She was like a hawk. I didn't care. It occurred to me that this pain was an answer to my prayers. Maybe I was sick. Yes, I would tell Miss Burke that I didn't feel well and ask to be excused.

The other girls continued squatting and straightening along with Miss Burke. I remained folded over. I groaned a little for effect, then staggered toward the bar along the wall. Behind me there were a few titters. One girl said, "Oh, gross!"

"Stop it, girls!" Miss Burke snapped.

I lifted my head and looked in the mirror. The exercises had come to a halt, though the music went on, and everyone was staring at me. What was the big deal? It wasn't as if I'd thrown up or anything. I turned to face them. I looked straight at Amanda, there in the first row, and she blurted out, "Elise, you've got *blood* on you."

I looked down at the front of my white leotard, at my black tights. Then I twisted my neck and peered into the mirror behind me. A red blotch spread across the seat of my leotard. I'd gotten my period.

I stood there dazed and amazed until Miss Burke barked something at the other girls, then led me into her office, a partitioned-off room in the back of the studio.

It was perfectly neat. There were no clothes strewn about, no books stacked in corners or winged open on surfaces as in my room. The small tapestry rug was perfectly aligned with the legs of the two hard wooden chairs, which were totally unsuitable for slouching. Even the contents of the cupboard Miss Burke opened were stacked and ordered.

Next to the cupboard stood a small table on which there was a photograph of a young woman. I thought maybe she was Miss Burke's sister, even though they looked nothing alike. The woman in the picture was blonde, like my mother and me. Her hair rippled and flowed around a heart-shaped face. She didn't have Miss Burke's hooked nose or the crease above it, but I pointed at the picture anyway and said, "Is that your sister?"

She jerked around to look at me, then turned back to the cupboard. "No. She was my student. She died in a car crash."

Poor Miss Burke. It seemed a lot of people in her life

had been killed in traffic accidents. I wanted to hear more, but she didn't seem in the mood for talking. She grabbed something off a shelf, then thrust a long, white pad at me. I fondled the pillowy napkin as she took a step toward the door. I realized that she didn't know it was the first time.

"Wait," I said.

She paused, on the edge of irritation. "Yes?"

"What do I do with this?"

"Put it between your legs."

And so I did. Alone, in Miss Burke's office, I wrestled out of my leotard and tights and then back into them, and spent the rest of the hour looking over Miss Burke's things.

At last, Mom burst into the room, breathless and panicky as if I'd been lost for a week. "Oh, darling!" she said. "Miss Burke told me. I can't believe it...so soon!" She flew at me and hugged me tight. Her skin, bared by the sleeveless dress she wore, was sticky from the heat. I caught a whiff of deodorant and perfume and skin. Underneath it all, there was this new smell coming from me.

"Listen," she said, "I'll walk right behind you until we get to the car and no one will see."

Back at home, Mom invited me into her bedroom for a private talk. I felt important as I plopped down on the chenille-covered bed. Amanda wasn't invited.

"I have no doubt," Mom began, "that you are going to blossom into a very lovely young lady."

I sat still, a warm joy filling me, waiting for her next words.

She took a deep breath, then went on. "And boys are going to want to touch you." Her gaze fluttered over my budding breasts then fell to the floor. She seemed very uncomfortable, but I couldn't tell if it was because of what she had to say or the changes in my body. Instinctively, I crossed my arms over my chest.

"Boys are going to want to touch you under your clothes," she said, her voice nearly a whisper, "but you mustn't let them. At least not until you're married."

I nodded. We'd already had our talk about the birds and the bees. At that time what she'd said had so repulsed me I'd vowed to stay a virgin forever.

She looked at me directly now. "Beauty isn't meant to be squandered. Do you understand?"

Although I didn't really, I nodded again, enraptured by the word "beauty." I knew that everyone considered Amanda the prettier of the two of us and I'd resigned myself to being the ugly duckling. Now Mom was telling me that I'd be a swan. Her words, her faith in the future stayed with me. I stored them in the back of my mind, in a safe place from which they could be taken out and marveled over at will. In the meantime, I made frequent trips to the bathroom to check on the blood. I was fascinated by the color of it and the strange new ache low in my belly. I had become a woman, while Amanda was still a little girl.

My birthday a month later took on a special significance. That year I would be celebrating a rite of passage as much as the anniversary of my birth.

A couple of weeks before, Mom asked me what I wanted for a present. I said, "Permission to quit dance school."

She scowled as if I'd made a sick joke. "Now, Elise, you've got to give it a chance. You've only been at it for a couple of months."

That first monthly flow had given me new ideas. I was older now, more mature, at least in body, and I thought I was old enough to start making decisions for myself. I wasn't a dancer and I never would be. And I couldn't be a mermaid, though maybe I could be a swimmer. I was beginning to realize that the dreams in my head were different from Mom's and it was time for me to sort them out and think about what I wanted to be.

"I'm not good at dancing," I said. "And Miss Burke knows it."

Mom sighed. "I've already paid for your lessons up until school starts. If you quit, it'll be money down the drain."

I backed down for the moment, determined to find another approach. Meanwhile, I learned to block out Miss Burke's frequent chastisements. My feet missed steps and stumbled, but my mind was somewhere else, riding waves, mingling with minnows.

For my birthday dinner, we were going all the way to Muskegon, twenty minutes away by car. Grand Haven didn't have a lot of restaurants, but in Muskegon there were Chinese restaurants, steak houses, and Pancho's, where the theme was Mexican. I chose that one, partly because I'd developed a liking for spicy food, and partly because I thought it might please my parents. I imagined they'd be able to conjure up memories of their trip to Mexico a few years earlier.

My birthday fell on a Tuesday. The restaurant was almost empty, so we could sit anywhere we wanted. There was a wide dining area with many tables, as well as nooks and corners that offered more privacy. A galaxy of Mexican decorations hung from the ceiling—piñatas, sombreros, dolls in bright clothes.

The dark-skinned, moustached waiter stood patiently by while I picked out a table. I chose one in the middle of the room where I imagined I'd be at the center of attention. The waiter handed us menus and lit the candle at the center of the table. The waxy stub was in a perforated tin can. Light flickered through the openings, making kaleidoscopic patterns on the tablecloth.

"What'll it be, señoritas?" Dad asked. "How about a quesadilla for my señora?"

Mom smiled indulgently. "Sure. That'll be fine."

My parents almost always ordered the same thing when we went out to eat. For a long time I'd accepted this as normal, thinking how good it was that Mom and Dad were so perfectly matched in taste. But now, for the first time, it occurred to me that Mom was deferring to Dad. She had designated him as lord and master and was willing to follow his lead, just as she expected me to follow hers. Well, that was it. I wasn't going to keep doing what she told me to forever.

I was famished by the time the waiter brought our food. I was immediately absorbed in my plate of tacos and beans, nearly oblivious, but not quite, to the other diners straggling into the restaurant. I noticed a family—mother, father, grandmother and two little boys, all dark complected like the migrant workers who picked blueberries in early fall. They were seated at a table near ours and their happy chatter almost drowned out the canned mariachi music.

"Are they speaking Spanish?" I asked in a low voice.

Mom cocked her head for a moment. "Yes, I believe they are."

As I had hoped, Dad launched into a remembrance of Acapulco, but I missed most of it because my eyes were on the couple who had just walked through the door. Of all the days in the year, and all the restaurants in Michigan, why did I have to see Miss Burke on my birthday? She was standing at the entrance, waiting to be seated. Her salt-and-pepper hair cascaded to her waist. I'd never dreamed it was so long. She wore a simple black dress that bared her thin, yet muscled limbs, sandals, and clunky silver bracelets. Even from this distance, I could sense a change. There was something soft and festive about her, totally unlike her studio persona.

At first I thought her companion was a man. The figure at Miss Burke's side wore baggy white trousers and a matching slouchy jacket over a black tank top. The face under the short thatch of hair was plain and free of makeup. But as the two moved away from the entrance, behind my parents and toward one of the ferned-in coves, I saw the jiggle of breasts under the tank top and decided she must be one of Miss Burke's dancer friends.

The two women were hidden from view, and although I was the only one who saw them, I was not about to draw attention to their presence. Mom would make us go over and greet them, and Amanda would probably start babbling about ballet. I looked quickly around the table to make sure Miss Burke had gone unnoticed, then I relaxed.

"...and the children eat little sugar candies shaped like skeletons," Dad was saying.

Mom shuddered dramatically. "Oh, let's not talk about that! Not on Elise's birthday."

Having found myself back in the conversation, I was disappointed. I loved hearing Dad talk about the Day of the Dead and all the other bizarre customs of Mexico.

I devoured chips and salsa and beans and tacos till I could feel the waistband of my skirt cut into flesh. I also drank two glasses of Coke. I excused myself to go to the bathroom before dessert.

I found the door marked "muchachas" with a skirted Mexican doll hanging from a tack. I recalled a movie in which a voodoo doll had been nailed to a door, and had a vague feeling of premonition before I went inside. The door opened with a soft whoosh. Someone was in one of the stalls. I could hear fabric rustling, zipper teeth parting. I stood listening, expecting the trickle of urine, but what I heard was wet smacking noises.

"This is madness," an oddly familiar voice gasped. "Someone might come in here."

And then the reply: "I don't care. I need to touch you."

I wasn't sure about what to do. I was obviously intruding on something, though I couldn't figure out what. This was the ladies room, after all—no men allowed. And I was pretty sure that those voices I'd heard belonged to women.

I bent down and looked under the door for legs. All of the stalls were empty, except one. There I saw white-trousered legs tangling with bare ones, sandals with thin straps and shiny black oxfords.

Then, that same voice: "Oh, do that again! Yes, like that!" So breathy, so rapturous, so unlike those dance school scoldings.

I heard cloth fall to the floor, the clatter of the toilet seat, and saw the crumpled white trousers on the bathroom floor. My bladder was about to burst, but I decided I could wait just a little longer. The door whooshed again as I made my exit.

It was hard to concentrate on the conversation back at the table and harder still to work up enthusiasm for the balladeer in a sombrero and serape who came to our table with his guitar. But I managed to smile while he strummed and sang "Happy Birthday to You." Our waiter brought out a dish of fried ice cream stuck with candles, and everyone applauded when I blew them out in one breath. I sat there dumbly. Only after Mom had plucked the candles from my dessert did I realize I'd forgotten to make a wish.

Mom finally spotted Miss Burke through the ferns as we were getting ready to leave. Naturally, she herded us into the private little enclosure where my dance teacher sat with her companion.

"What a surprise!" Mom said. "We're here celebrating Elise's birthday."

Miss Burke squirmed in her seat and forced a smile. "Happy birthday, Elise." Was it my imagination, or did she look ever so slightly disheveled? And wasn't her lipstick smeared?

A vision of Miss Burke and the woman now introduced as Maya flashed into my head: lacquered nails raking bare backs, a tango of tongues. My face filled with blood, and I dropped my eyes, wishing that I could click my heels like Dorothy in *The Wizard of Oz*.

In the car on the way home, Mom turned to Dad and said, "It's funny—when I saw Maya from the back I thought she was a man." She chuckled at her mistake, but I didn't think it was funny at all.

That night as I lay awake in bed, I couldn't stop thinking about Miss Burke. I remembered the photo in her office and the way she'd kissed Mom that first day in the studio. It came to me that I now knew her secret, and this gave me a sense of power I'd never had before. I didn't need ruby red slippers or birthday candles to make my wish come true.

The following afternoon I found Mom in the living room hemming a skirt. She was watching "Days of Our Lives," and at first I hesitated to interrupt her, but I knew that what I had to say was far more interesting than anything she'd see on TV.

"Mom?"

"Yes, honey?"

"I saw something...strange. Last night. In the bathroom at Pancho's." I stared at the floor, drawing figure eights on the carpet with my foot. When I glanced up, Mom was looking at me, her eyes brimming with concern.

"Something that upset you?"

"Well, yes."

"Why don't you tell me about it?" Her voice was gentle, a lullaby. I remembered how she'd always sweet-talked me out of fear after nightmares, and I felt a moment of guilt. I knew that what I had to say would shock her and hurt her far more than it did me. After all, she admired and adored Miss Burke. But her world was contained in boundaries of acceptable behavior. I knew that my words would hurt her. And maybe Miss Burke as well, but I also knew that this knowledge was a means to an end.

"I saw Miss Burke and Maya kissing in the bathroom," I said.

I didn't have to go back to dance class after that.

12

Of course Amanda had never stopped dancing, and was still dancing, but I was just beginning to figure out what kind of person I was going to be. My new identity was shaping up little by little. I was eager to try out my new hair and clothes in public, so I suggested Chiara and I ride our bikes to the waterfront.

"Good idea," she said. "I saw a Mexican restaurant downtown. I'm in the mood for something hot."

"You mean the Tip-A-Few?" I'd never eaten there before, but I'd heard it was a dive.

"Yeah," Chiara said, reading my mind. "Appearances can be deceiving."

I changed into pedal pushers and a T-shirt and we biked over the drawbridge, down leafy streets, to the corner of Maple and Main. We propped up our bikes and went inside.

Some guy with panther-black hair and dusky skin was playing a guitar, but it wasn't mariachi. I wasn't sure what to call that kind of music.

"Flamenco," Chiara said, over her shoulder.

We slid into a booth, but before we'd even ordered, Chiara was out of it, on the floor, dancing. She clapped in an erratic beat, her arms high in the air, her feet stomping. Her hips were like well-oiled ball bearings. We were in a third rate restaurant in a conservative Midwestern town, so I didn't think that it was likely anyone would join her. But another guy, who'd been sitting on the sidelines with a beer, suddenly got out of his chair and began moving toward Chiara with short, staccato steps. He clapped, too.

Someone called out "olé," and another began singing in a language I'd never heard before. Although I couldn't understand the words, I listened carefully as if sheer attentiveness would make them comprehensible.

Then I was aware of someone standing at the edge of the table. "I'll have a Coke and a beef burrito," I said, without looking up. Once again, I'd entered a sort of parallel reality with Chiara as my guide. Who knew that this sort of thing went on in Grand Haven?

Out of the corner of my eye, I saw the waitress approaching, and someone sitting down across from me.

"She'll have a Coke and a beef burrito," he said.

I looked in surprise and saw the Ferris wheel operator. He was wearing a flannel shirt with the sleeves cut off. His hair was loose, splayed over his shoulders.

"Um, hi."

"You're the one," he said, after the waitress had left with my order.

"What?"

"You're the one my mother told me about," he said, leaning forward. "She said I'd meet a gadje with grain-gold hair. Eyes the color of a lake in summer."

No man or boy had ever spoken to me like this before. I didn't know what to do. My face was burning, and I knew if I opened my mouth my voice would come out wavery and high, but I had to know: "What's a gadje?"

"That's what my people call anyone who's not Roma."

"Roma? You mean, Italian?"

"Gypsy."

"So, uh, your mom is a fortune teller?" I felt stupid as soon as I asked. Maybe he was feeding me a line, but no one had ever made that kind of effort before. I wanted to believe, even as I thought of my own mother, and how much she would disapprove. She thought that séances and Ouija boards were associated with Satan.

"Yeah, my mother has certain abilities," he said.

I liked his voice, the way it seemed to scrape along a gravel road.

He held out his hand, then. "I'm Miguel Ballesteros."

"Elise Faulkner." I gave him my hand.

He held it warm and tight in his for a moment before turning my palm face up. "This is me," he said, pointing to a hatch mark. "I'm your destiny."

I smiled and blushed again.

I looked out at Chiara. She was so vibrant, so present, that I couldn't believe every man in that room didn't want her. Eyes flew to that flaming hair, the dimples in her milky white cheeks. But when I checked Miguel, I saw that he was oblivious to her. He was staring at me.

"So how do you know it's me?" I asked. He could have been describing a million other corn-fed Midwestern girls.

He smiled. "I just know."

"Where do you go next?" I asked.

He shrugged. "Someplace in Ohio. I go where there's work. Sometimes I play music, sometimes I pick fruit. Once in a while I hook up with a carnival like this one. But I'll be seeing you again."

I wanted to hear what else was in store for us, but just then, the waitress brought my food, and Chiara, panting from exertion, started coming our way. He slipped away before I could introduce them. I never said anything to her about him because I was sure I'd imagined the whole thing.

13

Bethany Miller became Miss Coast Guard, and I paid my sister a dollar. The carnival packed up and moved on to another town. A little piece of my heart went along with it. I couldn't stop thinking about Miguel. What if he met someone else and realized that *she* was the girl with eyes the color of a summer lake that his mother had been talking about? What if I never saw him again?

Summer cooled into fall. On the first day of school, when Chiara got on the bus with me, a low rumbling of voices went from front to back like a wave. Already, she was causing a stir. There weren't any empty seats, so we had to double up.

Chiara strode confidently to the back where the gum-smacking, bra-strap-snapping boys usually sat and plopped down. I sat next to Christy Evans who got on a few stops earlier.

"Who's that?" she asked me.

"Chiara Hanover. She's staying with her grand-mother for a while."

"She's not from around here then, I guess. She sure looks weird." Christy was one of the crewneck and plaid wool skirt types that I'd once tried to imitate. Her smooth brown hair was held away from her face with a suede headband. Both her eyes were hazel.

"I think she's beautiful," I said.

Christy gave me a strange look, then turned to the window. We didn't speak for the rest of the ride. I looked out the window, trying to see the neighborhood with a newcomer's eyes. There was the motel whose manager had tried to kiss me when I babysat for his children. There was the fire station where two shiny red trucks waited for flames. What did Chiara make of the fire hydrants painted to look like dwarves? Did she think they were cute or silly? And what of Mr. Griffin, the retiree who spent entire days sitting in a lawn chair in front of his house watching the cars go by? He lifted his hand and waved as we passed by.

Chiara and I were in the same English and French classes. I wasn't sure why she was taking French since she'd lived in France, but I was glad I'd have someone to help me with assignments.

During French, while "Madame" Spencer was writing conjugations on the blackboard, Chiara sent a little paper airplane sailing through the air to my desk. It was such a blatant gesture that everyone in the class looked at her in open-mouthed surprise. Chiara just winked and put a finger to her lips. Mrs. Spencer turned to find a classroom full of conspiratorial smiles.

When no one was looking, I carefully unfolded the paper and read Chiara's scrawl: "Dites-moi de Matt Haines!"

Matt Haines? The boy that sat directly across from Chiara? He was the ultimate math geek. Why did she want to know about him? Maybe if his hair was feathered and not cut straight across his forehead, maybe if he wasn't so loose and gangly...

At lunch, as we sat side by side with our cafeteria trays, I asked Chiara, "Why are you interested in Matt? He's not popular at all."

She plunged a fork into her shepherd's pie. "Elise, do you think Baudelaire was popular in high school? Do you think Picasso dated cheerleaders?"

I was speechless. The first thing I was going to do when I got into study hall was find out who this Baudelaire was.

14

At school, I went from being invisible to being a topic of conversation. Whispers trailed me. The cheerleaders —those girls who lived in houses overlooking Lake Michigan, who shopped at boutiques in Grand Rapids—took note of Chiara and me. Their eyes roamed every thread of our new old clothes, every strand of our hacked-off hair. I couldn't have cared less. When I was with Chiara nothing mattered. *I am the great-granddaughter of Margaret,* I reminded myself. *I am the gadje with grain-gold hair.* Any day now, Miguel would show up on the school steps. Hadn't he promised that I'd see him again?

One day, Chiara and I were strolling down the hallway, on our way to English.

"Watch this," she said, as we approached Matt Haine's locker.

He was reaching up, trying to stuff yet another book into his locker. His highwater corduroys seemed even shorter when he stretched. There was hardly any room for the windbreaker crumpled into a crevice, not even hanging from the hook. Most kids had decorated the inside door of their lockers with magazine pictures of teen idols or big bold words cut from advertisements: Fresh! Just do it! Sexy. The only picture in Matt's locker was a sepia-toned postcard of Einstein on a bicycle.

Chiara waited until Matt had finished his business and closed the metal door. When he turned and was facing us, looking straight at us, in fact, Chiara winked at him. Then she continued walking down the hall.

I didn't move at first. I watched Matt, waiting for a bright blush to flood his cheeks, but he didn't seem embarrassed. His eyes followed Chiara, followed the slow swish of her skirt, the bounce in her walk, but they were filled with something like awe.

Chiara had no need of witchcraft or charms or magic love potions. That first wink was like a seed planted in Matt's heart. When he asked her out a week later, it was no big surprise.

The next morning, Amanda and I had breakfast together. Hers was a concoction of raw egg, yogurt, and wheat germ blended into froth and poured into a tall glass. This, and a weekly facial of honey-glued oats were two of the beauty secrets she'd gleaned from some magazine. While she sipped milliliter by milliliter, pretending to enjoy it, I ate my bowl of raisin bran. Dad had already made his exit, lunch box in hand. Mom was puttering around in the kitchen, washing up cups and spoons.

"Hey, what's that?" I asked, noticing a glint of gold on Amanda's left hand.

She stretched her arm across the table and splayed her fingers. A chip of diamond winked in the sun. "Clark bought it for me."

She'd told me before that he worked part-time bagging groceries.

"So what does it mean?"

"We're going to get married after graduation and live in a condo in Swiss Village."

I nodded, but I felt sick to my stomach.

"I've decided to go all the way with him," she whispered.

"What?" I dropped my spoon. We both listened to it clatter on the floor.

She repeated it, this time more confidently. "I love him and he loves me."

"But what if you get pregnant? Mom and Dad would have a fit. They'd die! They'd send you to Siberia."

She regarded me calmly. "We'll use a rubber."

This was not the way it was supposed to be. I was the big sister, she was the baby. I was supposed to be dispensing advice, handing out bits of wisdom gained from experience. In any other society, I would be courted first. As it was, I'd never been on a date.

Just then, the bleat of a car horn sounded in the driveway. "Oh, it's Clark!" she squealed, as if this were their first date, as if he hadn't been picking her up for school for the past two months. Chair legs scraped on linoleum as she pushed away from the table. She grabbed her book bag and dashed for the door.

Because I didn't have a boyfriend or a car, I would take the bus as usual. I didn't mind, especially since Chiara would be waiting at the bus stop. Plus, I needed to talk to her about this new development in my sister's love life. But when I got to the bus stop, backpack hitched over my shoulder, the girl was nowhere in sight. I had an awful vision of Matt swinging by in his second-hand car, whisking Chiara out of my life. I would have been waiting for the bus alone had it not been Randy, our next door neighbor. He was puffing on a Camel, holding the cigarette clipped between thumb and forefinger like a joint. His other hand clutched a brown paper bag. I'd never figured him for the sack-lunch type. He seemed more likely to escape campus to shoplift chips at convenience stores or to stuff himself at the McDonald's down the hill.

"Good morning," I said, brightly. It was just the two of us. Why not be friendly?

He nodded slightly, then blew a succession of smoke rings into the crisp morning air. He'd been barely civil since we got into high school, though we'd played in the sandbox together as kids. Randy was a stoner, one of the kids who slouched around the smoking area outside the school building between classes.

"What's wrong, your Mustang got a flat?" I asked.

"What's it to you?" His eyes were rimmed with red.

I shrugged. "Just making conversation."

The bus crested a hill and came into view. Randy flicked his cigarette into the dirt. Its tip glowed orange, and I thought of Smoky the Bear.

"Hey, where's your friend?" he asked.

"I don't know," I said. But I wished that I did.

"Give this to her, would ya?" He handed over the sack. It was all crinkly as if it had been wadded up and then ironed out with the flat of a hand. I was confused. Chiara and Randy knew each other? They were friends? What was going on here? And why was Randy giving away his lunch? But this was no sandwich. The bag was much too light.

Randy went to the back of the bus and I took a seat next to a curly-haired kid and opened the sack. There was a plastic bag inside containing what looked like grass clippings. I was about to pull it out for a better look when I realized what I was holding. My hand froze. I was a criminal. I quickly rolled the bag up, tucked it into my backpack, and looked around. The boy sitting next to me was staring out the window.

I wanted to unload this contraband, but Chiara wasn't at school. The place was lonely without her. I took my time twirling the dial of my locker and stuffing my jacket inside. I walked slowly down the hall to my first class, brushing past Shetland wool and corduroy. Everyone seemed to be watching me, eyeing my circa 1966 psychedelic dress. It was a genuine Pucci, though that wouldn't have made any difference to this crowd. They were all in Talbot's and Pappagallo and Brooks Brothers. There were murmurs and jeers as I walked by.

I sat through English and then physics. In pre-calculus, there was a test. I was almost finished—only two problems remaining—when there was a discreet knock on the door followed by some quick words between Mr. Scheffield, the teacher, and the school secretary.

Mr. Scheffield bent over my desk. "Elise, your mother has called you away. There's been some emergency in your family. You're to wait out in front of the school."

An emergency? A car accident? Heart attack? An image flashed into my mind—a glowing neon sign in the middle of the night, my footed pajamas with the rabbit applique. My mouth went dry.

"What about the test?" I asked dumbly.

"Don't worry. You can finish up tomorrow."

I shoved my paper and pencil aside, gathered my stuff, and stepped into sunshine and the cool of fall. My mother hadn't arrived yet. I wandered to the curb to keep watch.

A car was parked across the street, shaded by golden maples. It was boat-sized, shimmery blue, and vaguely familiar. Someone was sitting at the wheel. At first, the driver was only a silhouette, statue-still, waiting. Then, there was movement: wildly gesticulating hands, some kind of sign language. I stared. The driver leaned over and cranked down the window on the passenger side.

"Hey, stranger," she called out. "I've sprung you!"

"Chiara? What are you doing here? I'm waiting for my mother. There's been some kind of accident."

"Elise, you idiot, that was me. Nothing bad happened. Now get in the car."

I had no choice. There was no way I could walk back into school, back into math class. I boarded Mrs. Churchill's Cadillac. "What are you doing? We'll get into trouble. Besides, I was in the middle of a test. My grade depends on it."

Chiara put her foot to the gas pedal and the car lurched onto the road.

I pulled a safety belt across my lap.

"Relax. You should be thanking me. A little extra-curricular activity will do you good." She beamed a smile my way. "I don't see why you're so worried. You've gotten all As for the past three years, and your college applications are in the mail. Why not have a little fun?"

I shook my head in exasperation, knowing that I would go along with her every idea. I remembered the brown paper bag in my backpack. "And what's more, this morning I find out you've been making drug deals with Randy!" I pulled out the package and tossed it on her lap.

"Oh, goody!" she said. "I don't see why you're mad. I'm planning on sharing it with you."

It was no use. I'd have to give in. "So how did you get the car?" I asked.

"I told Grammy I wanted to look for a job after school, so she let me borrow her tank."

"You're really going to look for a job?"

She hooted. "Hell, no. Can you see me slinging burgers in this town? Or hawking pantyhose at Steketee's? Pas moi. I just thought it was about time we had a day off."

She pulled into a little take-out shop and we ordered a bag of fried clams, coleslaw, and French fries. Then we cruised out to the beach. We ate lunch while looking out at the silvery waves. In late fall, there were no sunbathers or swimmers, just sand and driftwood and the occasional pop can. A few gulls circled overhead. It could have been a desolate scene, but for me it was peaceful, even beautiful. I loved the lake, loved its suggestion of infinity. The water went on and on. As a child, I'd imagined foreign lands on that opposite shore—women in kimonos, maybe.

After our lunch, Chiara and I walked along the shore, past the hotel that was under construction, and then out onto the pier. A few men were fishing down near the big red lighthouse, buckets of bait at their feet. They fished the waters where the Grand River and Lake Michigan mingled. Across the harbor the white buildings of the Coast Guard shone in the early afternoon sunlight.

The pier was the site of my romantic fantasies. I longed to walk its length arm-in-arm with my lover, moonlight spilling over our faces. Of course there would be no fishermen as we kissed beneath the sequined sky. Until recently, I'd envisioned Clark as my companion, but now he didn't fit. Now I wondered what it would be like to stand here with Miguel.

Chiara and I had a perfect afternoon. We climbed the dune across the road and ran down it, giggling like children. We even played on the swing set. Happiness was so simple when I was with her.

"Thanks for today," I said, when she dropped me off at home.

She winked. "Stick with me, kid. The fun is just beginning."

15

When the letter from Kalamazoo College arrived, I sat on the edge of my bed for a long time, holding the unopened envelope. My heart pounded as I slit the envelope with my fingernail. I extracted the letter, noted the soft creamy vellum, breathed in the aroma of ink.

"Dear Ms. Faulkner," I read. "We are pleased to accept your application to Kalamazoo College..." I let the letter fall to my lap. Inexplicable tears filled my eyes. Months ago, this letter would have made me jump up and down. When I had been yearning to fling myself into the arms of adventure, I'd thought of college as my big getaway. But now that I was having such a good time, now that Chiara was my friend, I wasn't so sure.

I told Chiara the news that evening as we sat in her room, textbooks spread open on the floor, Billie Holiday's voice bleeding from the stereo speakers.

"That's great," she said. "Congratulations. I've heard Kalamazoo College is really cool. They have a great foreign study program. You'll meet lots of interesting people."

We were supposed to be studying for a French midterm, but Chiara was busy painting her toenails.

"Why don't you apply there, too?" I asked, suddenly hopeful. "We could be roommates."

She blew on her toenails, then held them up for my inspection. I nodded and smiled, but I was impatient to hear her answer.

"I don't think so, Elise. I'm not planning on going to college. At least not right away."

It had never occurred to me that she wouldn't be going at all. She was the brightest person I knew at Grand Haven High School. "What are you going to do, then?" I asked.

"I think I'll try being a writer," she said. "For that, I need life experience."

I thought she had enough of that already. "Will you at least apply?" I was nagging, but I felt desperate. What would I do without her? Who would be my guide?

She finally agreed to fill out the forms, but I could tell she was humoring me. Well, there was still time to make her change her mind.

"What about you?" she asked. "What do you want to be?"

I shrugged. "I don't know. When I was little I wanted to be a mermaid hunter."

Anyone else might have made fun of me, but Chiara nodded as if it was a logical career choice. "Tell me more."

"The idea came from my great-grandmother," I said. "Once, when she came up from being underwater, she told everyone that she'd seen a mermaid. Some people said that she'd probably seen a dead body floating around, or a fish, but she insisted."

"Do you believe she saw a mermaid?"

"I'd like to," I said with a smile. "I've read that people hallucinate when they're deprived of oxygen, so it was probably something like that. My grandmother, of course, believes that her delusion was more proof that she was crazy and unfit to be a mother. I guess that makes her feel better about having lost her mom."

Chiara got quiet, and I wondered if she was thinking about her mother, if she was missing her parents. I decided to change the subject. "Anyway, I always thought that I'd like to do something that involved travel or adventure."

I thought of Miguel then, running his finger over my palm in the Tip-A-Few. Had he been able to see my future occupation? Was it anything like I'd dreamed of? Would I go on trips? Would I dive under water?

As if she'd been reading my mind, Chiara said, "Well, get ready for adventure because this weekend we're going on a road trip."

"Here's the plan," Chiara said the next day at lunch. We leaned across the cafeteria table, huddled together like prisoners discussing an escape route.

Matt sat next to Chiara. He sat so close to her that his recently shorn hair brushed against her red locks. He was looking good, I had to admit. I marveled at the transformational power of love as I sucked down milk. Suddenly, other girls were noticing Matt's allure as well. Maybe they had finally realized that if Matt got into M.I.T. as planned, he'd turn out to be more wildly successful than all of their dream husbands put together. Or maybe they'd just discovered his sexy Elvis Presley pout, or the way his broad shoulders narrowed to compact hips.

It didn't matter, though, what other girls thought of him because he had tunnel vision when it came to Chiara.

"Here's the plan," she said again. "Elise, you tell your parents you're spending the weekend chez moi. I'll tell Grammy I'm staying with you."

"What if my mom calls your grandmother?" I could only imagine the punishment if I got caught. A hundred hours of community service? Confiscation of my library card?

"Elise," Chiara sighed heavily. "You worry too much. Live a little."

I decided to put my fears aside and listen to the rest of the plan.

"We'll have to leave right after school on Friday," Chiara said, "so bring clothes and whatever you need to school with you. Matt's going to drive his car."

That tin can? Matt's new fashion sense didn't quite extend to his car, which was painted various shades of primer. Not only was it ugly, but also it didn't look very durable. I wasn't sure it would make it to the corner without the muffler or something falling off, let alone all the way to Chicago.

That's where we were headed—Chicago. There was no decent jazz in Grand Haven, Chiara had declared more than once. Not even on the radio. So we were taking this secret road trip. It had taken weeks to arrange everything. First, we'd had to come up with fake IDs. Luckily, Matt knew someone with a laminator who had a veritable cottage industry going. We were soon the three proud owners of North Dakota driver's licenses, proclaiming us to be of legal age. I was 22, Chiara 23, and Matt, 25, which I thought was stretching it. He couldn't even grow a beard.

"It'll be dark," Chiara had said. "They'll never notice."

Next, we spent days debating what we would wear. Chiara, who'd been in jazz bars plenty of times before, was going to wear a fringed red dress worthy of a go-go dancer, with elbow length gloves. I'd decided on the black moiré dress I'd bought at Kiki's Closet, fishnet hose, heels, and a black beret. I had a black bag stitched with bugle beads to go with it.

That day after school, I told my mother I'd be spending the weekend with Chiara. It wasn't an outright lie.

"That's fine, honey. I'm so glad you girls have become such close friends." She had only recently recovered from The Haircut Incident. In the end, I think she was so eager for me to have a best friend like any other normal teenager that she decided to forget about the whole thing.

Friday morning I went to the bus stop with a bulging duffel bag. Chiara had already stashed hers in Matt's car the night before. She gave me a knowing look when she saw my bag.

"How'd it go with your parents?"

I gave her the thumbs-up sign. "They have the highest regard for your grandmother. They probably think we'll be playing Crazy Eights all weekend."

Chiara nodded. "Yeah, Grammy seemed thrilled I'd be out of her hair for a couple of days. I think she's planning some wild party."

I couldn't help laughing at the image of proper Mrs. Churchill unbuttoning one of her stranglehold blouses and letting down her blue-gray hair. It would be almost worth missing out on Chicago to see her twisting the night away on the Oriental rug.

16

I had been to Chicago before. The first time was with my parents to visit Mom's aunt and uncle. To me, Aunt Audrey was sophisticated and glamorous with her dyed-brown pageboy and moist red lips. Cigarettes had made her voice raspy. At Aunt Audrey's house, dinner was served late—an hour past my usual bedtime. After dinner, she and Uncle Pete took us to different places in the city. I remembered hotel lounges with piano players, the gigantic planes taking off from O'Hare, the dazzle of city lights in a black night. To my little-girl mind, Chicago was a city of promises and adult privileges. As I sat eating peanuts from a napkin, Cole Porter songs swelling around me, I could forget that I was just a kid, eleven going on twelve.

On that trip, Mom, Dad, Amanda and I had spent the three-hour car ride singing and playing games. We kept track of out-of-state license plates, picked out the alphabet on billboards and neon signs. We sang "Row, Row, Row Your Boat" in rounds.

This time, there was no singing and no games. I sat in the back of Matt's rust-eaten car while Chiara sat up front, cuddled against Matt's red sweater. The radio was turned on, and as the music floated back to me, I watched the cornfields blur through the window. I was excited, but I held my feelings close.

Lake Michigan was swallowing the sun by the time we reached the city. Our plan was to first check into a cheap motel then go out to dinner. We'd already decided that Chiara and Matt would stay together, and I would have my own room. We were going to divide the cost three ways to be fair.

"What about the Holiday Inn?" I suggested. I wouldn't have minded staying somewhere with a pool and room service, even if I couldn't take advantage of them.

"Oh, Elise. You're so bourgeois." Chiara rolled her eyes at me. Then she smiled broadly to show that she was kidding.

We finally decided on a hotel wedged between a butcher's shop and a Chinese laundry. At that time of day, the street was deserted. Business hours were over and an eerie quiet had settled upon the district. I felt a shiver run down my spine. We'd left the safety of the suburbs.

The hotel lobby was dimly lit. A man in a T-shirt sat behind the registration desk. When he asked us to sign in, he spoke with a foreign accent. He took our money and handed us keys to neighboring rooms.

I went into mine and was pleased to find it neat and clean, although none too luxurious. There was a picture of a vase full of roses above the bed. A slight odor of cigarettes hung about the room. The walls were thin. I could hear Chiara and Matt opening and shutting closet doors, flushing the toilet, and laughing in the room next door. A radio played softly. For a moment, I was misted in loneliness and I wondered why I'd come. I sat down on a hard wooden chair and looked out the window. In a doorway across the street, a woman did little dance steps to warm herself. Her legs were bare, but she clutched a furry coat around her torso. She was wearing high heels. When she moved into the light of the street lamp, I saw that her makeup was as garish as a clown's.

The sound of fists on wood distracted me.

"Are you ready?" Chiara called.

I went to the door, unbolted it, and let her in. Instead of the sophistication I'd expected, our adventure was making my friend even more bouncy and childlike. She couldn't hold still. The fringes on her dress quivered with her every movement.

I took my time pulling on the fishnet stockings, scenting my wrists with Chanel No. 5 borrowed from Mom's vanity, shimmying into my dress. Chiara sat on the bed smoking a cigarette and tapping her foot. I only half-listened as she rattled off a list of places we'd visit. I was trying to imagine myself into a new persona—a city girl with sass, a Midwestern Dorothy Parker.

When the last zipper had been zipped, the last stroke of lipstick applied, we set off into the crisp evening. The wind off the lake lashed at our hair, and left bright red spots on our cheeks. In spite of the chill, we would walk to our destination and take a taxi back later. The idea of taking a cab for the first time was thrilling for me, but I affected nonchalance. I was careful not to throw my head back and marvel at the heights of buildings.

We ate dinner in a little basement Italian restaurant. The small dining room was crowded with tables. Laughter and conversations in Italian and English rang out. When we sat down at a corner table, I had the sense we were joining a lively party.

Matt ordered a carafe of red wine. The waitress took a quick look at our North Dakota's driver's licenses and then brought out three glasses.

"Isn't this great?" Chiara said. "We're going to have a ball tonight."

We ate up plates of spaghetti, drank the wine, sopped up the sauce with big chunks of bread. It was nine o'clock by the time we paid our bill and climbed to the street. Chiara said that we were ready for music. Warmed by wine, I happily followed her to our next stop.

We flashed our IDs at the Blue Parrot, a jazz bar a few blocks away. As soon as we entered I could feel the bass notes vibrating my breastbone. Through a haze of cigarette smoke I could see a quartet at the back—men in loose suits making love to their instruments. The pianist's hands flew over ebony and ivory with a mad passion. The trumpeter's body swayed like a snake charmed out of a basket. The light caught his puffed cheeks, making them glow like polished apples. Another man, eyes hidden by shades, held a bass as if it were his dance partner. Standing back, waiting for his moment to jump in, was the sax player.

We settled at a table near the stage and ordered drinks. I asked for a daiquiri, although I had no idea what it was. I liked the name; it sounded French. Chiara and Matt ordered bourbon on the rocks. They sat with knees touching, fingers entwined, but Chiara kept flashing me smiles, drawing me into her pleasure. The music was too loud for conversation. We gave in to the syncopated sounds, the saxophone playing straight to the heart.

I sipped my daiquiri, enjoying the taste of lime and the rush of rum, while Chiara danced in her chair. Matt bobbed his head, displacing strands of slicked-back hair. He worked to peel the cellophane from a fresh pack of Marlboros, ripped open the paper, and pulled out two cigarettes. He put them both between his lips and lit them with one match. Then he passed one to Chiara.

I imagined another pair of hands, a silver lighter snapped open as I held a cigarette between black-gloved fingers. Someone like Jay Gatsby in the book we were reading for English class, someone dapper and charming, appealing to my companion with a little bow: "You wouldn't mind if I danced with your lady, old sport, now would you?" Across the room Daisy would be dancing, swaying her knees to the music of a swing band.

Chiara touched my hand. "Isn't this doing it for you?" she asked, jerking her head toward the musicians.

I smiled and nodded my head, trying to convey that I was having fun, that she had chosen a good place, that I did not want to leave. But she wanted to see me entranced by music, elevated a few inches above the world.

"We'll go someplace else," she mouthed.

My protest was lost under the bass notes.

We finished our drinks and when the quartet took a break, we wrapped ourselves in coats and headed for the door.

The cold hit me smack in the face. I wanted to go back into that dark den where I knew it was warm, but Chiara pulled me along by my sleeve.

"I know of another place I think you'll like," she said. "It's just around the corner."

The streets were strangely quiet. We walked for a couple of blocks until we reached an inconspicuous doorway. There was no neon sign, no bouncer, nothing to indicate that we were entering someplace special. But Chiara had confidence and we trusted the map of Chicago in her head.

Matt and I followed her down wooden stairs into a space no bigger than the living room in my house. A bar stood off to one corner. Posters from old European movies papered the walls. There was no furniture to speak of, except for an unoccupied stool at one end of the room. Thirty or forty people stood around with drinks as if they were guests at a cocktail party. The only music came from speakers hanging from the ceiling.

"A drink?" Matt asked.

I nodded distractedly. This wasn't the kind of place I'd expected Chiara would lead us to. The floor was concrete. Spicy smoke hovered in a cloud above heads. I stood at the center of that room trying to understand what we were doing in that place with no jazz while dark-eyed men and women with black lipstick swarmed around me. A woman wearing a vinyl dress glanced at her watch.

"What is this place?" I asked Chiara.

She smiled. "You'll see."

Matt appeared and put a plastic cup in my hand. "Beer."

"Thanks."

He turned to Chiara and put an arm around her waist. As he pressed his lips to her neck, I was distracted by the sudden movement of the crowd. I moved with them, toward the stool, until I was at the edge of a pool of light. Then a door that I hadn't noticed before opened and a man carrying a guitar stepped into the room. He was tall and slender, his shoulders shawled by straight black hair. I could see the muscles flexing and rising under worn denim as he moved to the stool. He wore a white blouse befitting a pirate, sashed with a red silk scarf. His long face, balanced by a Roman nose, was slightly darkened by the vestiges of beard.

I felt a sudden urge to rub my cheek against his and to hide my head under that curtain of glossy hair. And then I saw his eyes and my heart stopped. I'd seen those eyes before. This man was my carnie. This was Miguel.

I stood frozen, barely breathing. The room became still and silent. He propped the guitar on his knee and started to play.

At first his fingers plucked at single strings like a spider climbing its web. The notes in a minor key, long and plaintive, brought forth a sadness in me. He was playing away wounds, I thought. I wanted to salve them, to infuse his fingers and his heart with sweetness and joy.

The melody slowed and one note lingered as his fingers paused. Not a breath could be heard, only that pure aching note. Miguel looked up from his guitar to the faces turned toward him. His eyes moved slowly. No one moved.

His gaze landed on mine, caught, and held. My world was suddenly reduced to twin brown orbs and the thumping of my own heart. Then, eyes still on mine, his fingers began moving faster and I realized that the quickening music was a language. He was speaking to me, making promises, begging the same from me. Faster and faster his fingers flew. His fierce strumming filled the room.

Around me, people began moving. Out of the corner of my eye, I could see a young woman dancing. I stood still, rapt, until Miguel's hands hushed the strings and his eyes fell away from mine. And then I clapped until my palms stung.

He nodded, his face a mask of pride. He held his chin high as he swept his eyes over the young women with dyed hair and the earringed men. He looked at me once more, but only for a second. When he dropped his eyes, he smiled privately and began to play again.

He gave us songs long into the night, saying only a few words in between, as if he preferred the eloquence of his guitar. And then he stopped, stood, bowed in a courtly manner, and disappeared behind the door again.

I wanted to chase after him, bust down the door if need be. I wanted to tell him my secrets, tear that white cotton from his shoulders and run my tongue over his bare skin. I'd never felt this jolt of attraction before and it unsettled me. Desire had come to me, quick and strong.

"Last call!"

I brought my hands to my ears, meaning to shut out the chatter and laughter that were pushing away my dream. I wanted to stay in that trance-like state. The lights were suddenly too bright, the rock music now spewing from the speakers unworthy of my ears. I stared at the door.

Chiara appeared at my elbow. "I saw you," she said breathlessly. "You looked like you were in another world."

"I was." I touched her arm in a feeble expression of gratitude. She had brought me to this place, after all. I owed her.

"Do you want to go out for breakfast?" she asked. "I know of an all-night diner that has great hash browns. It's only a block away."

It was nearly three a.m. I should have been tired, maybe even hungry, but I didn't want sleep or food. "No, thanks," I said. "I think I'll go back to the hotel. You two go ahead."

She wrinkled her brow. "Are you sure?"

"Absolutely. I'll get a cab." I tried to quell her big sister impulses with a smile. "Don't worry! Go on! Scat!" I shoved her away with both hands.

Chiara and Matt put their coats on, linked arms, and headed for the door. I was stuck in place, straining to hear something from beyond that other door, hoping it would open.

I took a step toward it, wondering what I would say to him if he came out. What if he didn't remember me? What if all that stuff about fate was just a bunch of crap? What if this was just a one-in-a-million chance encounter? I moved slowly until I was close enough to kiss the wood and then I knocked. The door stood firm and solid—a barrier. I wanted to kick it, or attack it with a chainsaw. Instead, I knocked again.

The music was loud. Twangy electric guitars and frenetic drumbeats drowned out any words he might have spoken, any possible rustle of fabric indicating his presence. Maybe he couldn't hear my knocking.

I palmed the doorknob and closed my fingers around it. "Please," I whispered. The doorknob turned in my hand. Another hand clamped down on my shoulder.

"What do you think you're doing?"

I looked up to see the bartender looming over me and felt his hot breath on my face. "Isn't this an exit?" I asked, feigning ignorance.

He shook his head. "It's the dressing room. You're not allowed in there."

"Oh, sorry." I turned away from him and dragged my feet to the other door. Maybe I was wrong. Maybe it wasn't my Miguel. After all, Chiara hadn't seemed to recognize him, and I'd had a lot to drink. I wanted to sit down on the curb and cry. I had no idea how to flag down a cab. A long, solitary walk back to the hotel would suit my brooding better, I thought, but if my mother was right, the city was seething with rapists and murderers.

The streets were deserted. Not even the hookers with their slit skirts and rouged cheeks remained. I started walking.

I had only gone a few blocks when I heard footsteps clicking on the concrete behind me. An involuntary shudder ran down my spine and I quickened my pace. The footsteps became faster. The hotel was near, on the next block. I only had to make it past the sign that promised "Checks Cashed Here," past the music store with the banjo hanging in the window. I started running. In my mad dash, I left behind one spiky-heeled shoe, tripped, and fell to my knees, rending my stockings and tearing my skin.

I was caught. I couldn't get away. I would die. And then I looked up and he was standing there, reaching a hand out to me.

"Elise," he said. "Why didn't you wait?"

Even before he pulled me to my feet, I knew what was going to happen. I had a sense of giddy inevitability heightened by drink and fatigue. My mother's voice was banished from my head. I invited Miguel up to my room.

The front desk clerk was watching television. He kept one eye on the black-and-white movie as he fumbled for the key to my room. I held it like a treasure against my chest and led the way up the dimly lit stairs.

Inside the room, Miguel bent down and said, "Let me have a look at this knee."

It was bleeding, but I didn't care. I let him peel the stockings down my legs, shivering at the slightest touch. Finally, I couldn't stand it any longer. "Just kiss me," I said. And I opened myself to him.

I was exhausted, but I didn't want to sleep. Not yet. "Talk to me," I said. "Tell me a story."

Miguel was silent for a long moment, but then he shifted into a more comfortable position and began to speak. "Close your eyes," he said. And I did. With my head on his chest, I could feel his words vibrating against my cheek.

"Long, long ago, when our people had no instruments, there lived a beautiful maiden in the forest. She had golden hair, like you, and blue eyes, and her cheeks were always plump and rosy. Everyone agreed that she was the fairest, by far, of any woman in that region, but she was a little crazy and so no one would marry her.

"This girl was in love with the young man who lived next door. Madly in love. He was handsome and serious and strong as a bear. The girl wandered the forest whispering his name and yearning for love.

"One day, she came across a creature, part man, part goat. There were horns coming out of his head and a scraggly beard hanging from his chin. 'Hello there, young maiden,' he said in a deep, dark voice. 'Why do you wander the forests so?'

"The girl wrung her hands together and looked at the creature with tears in her eyes. 'I am in love to the point of despair with the young man who lives next door, but he will not even look at me.'

"'Is that all?' The creature snorted and pawed at the ground with his cloven hoof. 'If you do one small thing for me, you can marry him and live happily ever after.'

"'And what might that be?' the girl asked, wiping away her tears.

"'Give me your mother and father and I will make that young man fall deeply in love with you.'

"'Then they are all yours,' she said, without hesitation. She did not hate her parents. No, nothing like that. It was her madness that made her betray her parents so easily.

"The creature turned her father into a guitar and her mother into its strings. Then he handed the instrument to the girl and said, 'All you have to do is play this and that swain will be yours.'

"The creature disappeared and the girl sat down on a log and began to play. The forest was filled with such beautiful music that even the rabbits and squirrels and deer gathered to listen. The birds paused in their singing.

"The young man heard the music, too, and of course, fell in love and married the girl. They spent their evenings singing and dancing in perfect joy. This continued until one afternoon when they were in the forest gathering berries. The girl laid the guitar under some bushes, but when they had filled their buckets with woodland fruit, it was no longer there. They searched and searched and finally gave up. As they were walking home along a dirt road, heads hanging with disappointment, a carriage drawn by four black horses appeared in a cloud of dust. The girl and her husband were whisked away by the goat man and no one ever saw them again.

"Much later, a little Gypsy boy playing in the forest accidentally stumbled onto the hidden guitar. He plucked at its strings and was amazed by the beautiful sounds that swelled up around him. It was like the harp of angels, he thought, and he took the guitar back to the camp where his family lived. Of course, everyone was delighted with this wondrous treasure and the Gypsies have loved music and dancing ever since."

When Miguel's story ended, I opened my eyes expecting to see trees all around me, but there were only the murky shapes of hotel furniture. "It's kind of sad," I said, thinking of the girl and her husband. I remembered Chiara's words: "Love is a crazy thing." I thought of Miss Burke, and my sister, and I wondered if it was love that had made me open myself to this man that I barely knew. "Tell me another one," I said. "A story with a happy ending."

But he was silent. He stroked my hair until I fell asleep and dreamed of a little boy kicking up sticks and pine needles. A little Gypsy boy named Miguel.

17

Bam! Bam! Bam!

"Elise! Wake up! Are you in there?"

I opened my eyes. My eyeballs were dry and sore. The bed next to me was empty, the sheets splotched with blood. Miguel was gone, leaving only a few strands of hair behind on the pillow, which I coiled in my palm. I was only half-disappointed. What I really wanted to do was lie in bed all day and replay the past several hours in my head. Or better yet, I'd start with my first sight of him at the Ferris wheel, the zap as we touched, on to the Tip-A-Few, his finger on my palm, to him sitting on the barstool, to his fingers gliding over my skin like water spiders. I didn't want to talk about it, at least not yet. I would probably tell Chiara later—after all, she was my best friend—but for now, I wanted to keep everything to myself.

"I'm here," I croaked.

"Hurry up and get out of bed." Chiara's voice was muffled by the door. "It's almost one and we're starving."

All through lunch, I could see the questions in her eyes. She could tell I had a secret. Maybe she'd heard something—a thump, a cry. I raised my eyebrows back at her. Had she and Matt...? There would be plenty of time for talk later. For now, we were busy with our thick-crust

S U Z A N N E   K A M A T A

pizza, looking forward to visiting the art museum.

"So what'd you think of that guitar player?" Chiara asked between bites.

"Awesome," Matt said. "The next Django Reinhardt, if you ask me."

I nodded, hoping that the heat I felt in my face wasn't a giveaway blush. "He was really good."

"He looked kind of familiar," Chiara said, cocking her head.

I could have told her then, and she would have remembered, but I didn't say anything. The talk turned to jazz. Matt and Chiara chattered excitedly about their favorite musicians and I launched into a daydream.

It wasn't until we'd downed our last swigs of Coke that I discovered I had no money. The bills that had nestled in my wallet the night before were gone. In their place was a folded cocktail napkin with the words, "I'll see you again," in bleeding ballpoint ink. Adrenaline rushed through my veins. I smuggled the napkin into my jeans pocket and showed the empty wallet to my friends.

"Hey, guys. It looks like I've been robbed."

Chiara frowned. She must have found my smile weird. Only a nutcase would be happy about being stolen from. But the truth was, I didn't care. For all I knew, someone had snuck into my purse while I'd stood listening to Miguel play. And even if he'd taken the money, about fifty dollars, I didn't care. It was his. I would have given it to him if he'd asked. Chiara said, "But we'll have to go easy on the beer tonight. Was your fake ID ripped off, too?"

I thumbed through my cards. "No. It's still here." It would be another few days before I discovered that my real driver's license was missing.

Chiara slid me a twenty across the table and sighed. "This puts a definite glitch in our plans," she said. "No

102

more taxis."

I didn't mind walking, and I didn't mind taking the bus. I was floating along, but not really in the moment. I stood in front of Serraut's *Sunday Afternoon in the Park* staring blindly at points of color, but my mind was on the secret soreness between my legs. That evening we once again made the rounds of clubs. We even went to the basement room where we'd seen Miguel play, but another performer was on stage.

The next morning, we gathered our stuff and set out for home. We barely had enough money to put gas in the car and buy breakfast at McDonald's. We'd spent our energy, too, so I was glad to be Michigan-bound, napping in the back seat.

Back in Grand Haven, Matt dropped Chiara and me off a block away from home. We stashed our bags in the bushes and, unencumbered, started up Mrs. Churchill's driveway.

My mind was in a dingy Chicago hotel room. My legs moved automatically as I trudged behind Chiara. I kept my eyes down. I didn't see a thing.

"Oof!" Chiara said, when I bumped into her. She'd stopped in her tracks.

I finally looked up and saw a shiny red Porsche parked ahead. I started to speak, but Chiara gave me the answer before I could get the words out.

"My father's here." She didn't smile.

We stood there for a long moment. I wondered what had brought on this surprise visit and if it had come about before or after our disappearance was discovered. For surely they knew by now, my parents and Mrs. Churchill, that we had not been "sleeping over." I wondered if anyone had called the police. And then, wildly, illogically, I wondered if I would be sent to jail. Lies and alibis collided in my head like bumper cars.

Finally, Chiara sucked in a deep breath and forced a smile. I'd never seen her scared before. "So do you want to meet him?"

What I really wanted to do was dash down the hill and burrow into a hole, at least until graduation. Instead, I matched her smile and said, "Sure."

She started whistling a cheerful tune and we covered the few yards to the door. I half-expected a guillotine to slice through me when we crossed the threshold, but we were met with only silence. At first I thought the house was empty—it was church time, after all—and I heaved a sigh of relief. In the kitchen, china cups and saucers sat in the sink waiting to be washed: a sign of hospitality. I started to count the cups and spoons. Mrs. Churchill called out from the depths of the house.

I trailed Chiara to the parlor. Her grandmother was there, of course, holding court, and so were my parents. Mom was dressed in one of her pastel suits that she wore when she went out to lunch. She was wearing lipstick and heels and her expression was as severe as her pulled-back hair. She looked like a volcano about to erupt. Dad sat next to her, looking sad. He shook his head slightly when I walked in, the way he did when the Tigers lost a ball game. I felt myself growing smaller and smaller.

There was someone else in the room filling the chair where I had first found Chiara. His large but trim body spilled over the velvety cushions. A pair of Ray Bans were pushed back on his head, as if to keep strands of thick beach-blond hair from falling into his eyes. His toned physique suggested seasons of sports - racquetball, skiing, tennis. He didn't rise out of the chair to greet his daughter, didn't draw her into an embrace, but he didn't seem particularly angry. In that room of poker faces, he actually smiled, revealing a row of perfect teeth. Here was a man who had no worries, a man in perfect control of his world.

"So *there* you are," he said good-naturedly.

It was then that I noticed the half-empty Jack Daniels bottle on the low coffee table. The whiskey bottle that Chiara kept beneath her bed.

10

"Dear Elise,

"Timber Hills is a drag, but if I want to hang on to my trust fund, I have to do penance. Que sera, sera, as they say. The best part is group, where everyone bares their souls and divulges the most interesting secrets. You'd be amazed at what some people have done for a glass of Scotch. One woman confessed to drinking a Chanel No. 5 cocktail. Another one actually stole from her children. I'm getting lots of ideas for my novel.

"Hope you're not too bummed out by what happened. At least you didn't have a baggie of pot in your locker at school. I've been a bad, bad girl, n'est-ce pas? I guess Santa will be filling my stocking with coal this year. Well, keep your chin up and if you ever start thinking your life is bad, remember Billie Holiday!"

Chiara had been gone for a month, and I missed her like crazy. This was her first letter from the rehab center, and I read it over and over, trying to conjure her voice and that glint in her different-colored eyes.

Her departure had cut through me like betrayal. My Chiara wouldn't succumb to a bribe, I thought. My Chiara would kick and scream and start some glorious revolution. She wouldn't climb meekly into her father's sports car and flutter her fingers as they pulled out of the driveway. I was disappointed, my spirit was bruised. But most of all, I was lonely.

When I wasn't angry at her for giving in, I was plotting her escape. I thought about how I'd trick the receptionist with some sister story, sneak into hospital garments, and pretend to be a nurse taking Chiara out for her constitutional. Then there was the Greyhound getaway, the peroxided hair and new names. Passage to Canada.

I was sure that Chiara didn't belong in a rehabilitation center. And I couldn't stand the idea of a newly reformed Chiara preaching about the dangers of alcohol. I'd had a taste of adventure and I knew I wanted more. And I wanted her to be with me. In the meantime, I was under house arrest.

Throughout that long afternoon, I kept waiting for the ax to fall. I knew there would be consequences galore and I wanted to know what they were, but Chiara's father persisted in small talk—the gas mileage of his Porsche, the weather in Spain, the greens at the local country club. Mom, I knew, was too well-mannered to throttle me in front of a stranger. That would come later. And it wasn't until later that I found out about Chiara's fate.

She didn't show up at school the next morning. Matt and I ate lunch together and pondered the situation.

"It must be bad," I said. "She didn't call me either." I pictured her in Mrs. Churchill's attic, surviving on bread and water.

That night while I was drifting between dreams, I woke to a scratching sound, like branches stroking the windowpane. When I heard my name softly spoken, I bolted upright and scrambled out of bed and to the window. In the next bed, Sleeping Beauty's slumber went undisturbed. The red luminous numbers on my clock radio registered 2 a.m.

Chiara was dancing on the lawn. She looked like some woodland nymph paying homage to the moon. Her thrift shop coat was unbuttoned, revealing glimpses of the long thermal underwear she slept in. She was wearing combat boots, but her movements were as light as a ballerina's.

I crept out of my room and out of the house to meet her.

She told me what had happened.

"Basically, I have two choices. I can go and live with my father and his child-bride, or I can go to a rehab center and get 'dried out.'"

"But you're not an alcoholic," I said. "How can they send you to rehab?"

Chiara shrugged. "I don't know. But I've heard it's like camp. You do arts and crafts and sit around telling stories. It doesn't sound so bad, and anything would be better than living with Bridget."

"What about your mother?"

Chiara shook her head. "Mom's a mess. She drinks and does drugs and has way too many lovers. If I go back to her, Dad will sue for custody."

"You're almost eighteen," I argued.

She put a hand on my shoulder. "Listen, kid. My parents are not reasonable people. If I don't do what my father says, I lose my inheritance."

My sentence was a little lighter. I was grounded for the next three months. I wasn't allowed to go to parties, to go out with friends, or to even venture beyond the yard after school until March. I didn't care. As long as the letters kept coming, nothing else mattered. I insisted on getting the mail every day and I suppose Mom considered it a concession.

The first missive was a postcard tucked between a packet from Publisher's Clearing House and the telephone bill. I studied the picture on the front—enormous Clydesdales draped with Budweiser banners—then flipped it over to read the back:

"My dear Elise, you asked for a happy story and so here it is. Once upon a time there was a lone Gypsy who traveled from town to town. Every night he played his guitar, hoping to summon his one true love. He found her again in the City of Wind. Miguel."

It was postmarked St. Louis, Missouri, but there was no return address. Maybe he had no itinerary, didn't know where his Gypsy feet would take him.

I had never given him my address. At first, I imagined that he'd found it in a crystal ball, but then I remembered the missing driver's license. He must have kept it. It pleased me that he carried my picture with him. I only wished that I had one of him. I was desperate for a more certain link.

I thought that if his mother could see into the future, then maybe he could receive communications by other means. I sequestered myself in my room and, thinking it an appropriately mystical posture, arranged my limbs in the lotus position. Eyes closed, breath deepened, I concentrated on Miguel.

"Can you hear me? I'm waiting for you. I love you, Miguel. I'll love you till the end of time."

I didn't write any of this down. I wouldn't take the risk of having Mom or Amanda find out about it. But without a written account, I was afraid of forgetting even a second of the time we'd spent together. And if I forgot the golden flecks in his eyes or the way the hair on his arms gently curled, I would be devastated.

I was reading the second letter, postmarked Kansas City, for the third time when Amanda burst into the room.

Her eyes were puffy and red from crying. Tears had

washed away her mascara, which was now streaked down her cheeks. She looked hideous.

"What happened?" I folded my letter carefully, secretly relieved that she was too upset to have the slightest interest in my mail.

"I want to die," she blurted. She threw herself across her bed and embraced her pillow.

"You break a fingernail?" Nothing seriously bad had ever happened to Amanda before. This behavior was new and interesting.

"You know, Elise, you can really be a bitch."

Then it dawned on me. Something had happened with her wonderful boyfriend, the one she was going to marry and live with happily ever after in Swiss Village. "Clark?"

She began writhing furiously as if she wanted to get out of her perfect skin. The bedsprings creaked in protest.

"Well, what did he do?" I asked.

"He broke up with me," she sobbed. She yanked a tissue from the box next to her bed and blew her nose indignantly. "Can you believe it?"

Over the next hour, I heard the grim tale of Amanda's abandonment. It came out in bits and pieces, punctuated by hiccups and sobs and froggy gulps. There was something about her sad posture and her utter disregard for her smeared makeup that touched my heart. A few months earlier, I would have been happy about this break-up. I would have seen it as my chance. But now I thought that Clark wasn't worthy of me or my sister. I was even more convinced of this as she told me about Lena Hartman.

Lena was the girl Clark had dumped my sister for. I knew her by reputation only. She didn't go to Grand Haven High School, but to our rival school in Spring

Lake, across the river. Lena was larger than life—a leggy, sun-bleached blonde in a red convertible. She'd done some modeling in Grand Rapids and word had it that she was going on to bigger and better things in Tokyo and Milan. I was quite sure that in no time Lena would move on to someone else and Clark would come crawling back to Amanda. I was going to make sure she didn't take him back.

"I know it hurts now," I said, "but in a couple of years you'll be glad this happened."

Amanda's bloodshot eyes beamed disbelief.

"Look at it this way. One day you'll run into him at homecoming and Clark will still be a bag boy at Meijer's Thrifty Acres while you're living the good life in Silicon Valley."

"But I don't want to live in Silicon Valley," she wailed.

She was still married to her vision of those condominiums with their cheap shag carpeting. I shook my head in disgust.

Just then, Mom, who I'm sure had never had her heart broken by a boy, came in carrying mugs of hot chocolate. Amanda, morose as ever, held hers in her lap but didn't drink. Mom sat on the edge of the bed and smoothed the hair back from her face. "There, there," she said. "Everything will be all right. He'll probably call you tomorrow and apologize and everything will be like before."

I rolled my eyes, thinking that all my hard work was going down the drain.

"Why don't you and Elise go shopping this weekend? You can take my credit card."

My ears perked up. What was she saying? Was she going to let me out of the yard? I held my breath, sure that Amanda, with a petulant shake of her head, would quash my chance of a reprieve.

Instead, she turned her head on the pillow and looked at me. "Do you want to go, Elise?" Sniffle, sniffle.

"Sure," I said, trying to sound casual. "If you like."

The problems of the world solved, Mom brightened and stood up to leave. And so thanks to Amanda and Clark, I would be able to spend my Saturday as a free woman.

Mom sat down on the sofa next to me the following afternoon. I could tell by her tentative manner that she had prepared "words," that she was trying to be delicate. "Elise," she began. Her voice was gentle, sweet.

I didn't want to listen, but I knew that if I gave her my attention and pretended to agree with everything she said, she'd soon go away.

"I know that you think we're being harsh," she said, "and I know that your little escapade was Chiara's idea—"

"I wanted to go," I interrupted. And I would do it all over again. I would not have missed that music, those lips and fingers, for anything.

Mom sighed, but she was not to be deterred. "Well, maybe you did want to go. That's not the point. The thing is, Elise, you're almost an adult and you have to start thinking about responsibility. You can't, for example, just go running off to Chicago without a care in the world."

And then I remembered the bus ticket buried in silk. The one in Mom's drawer. The one to Indiana. I wondered if it was still there, yellowed, frayed by sentimental fingerings.

"Terre Haute," I mumbled. "June 15, 1974."

"What?" Her face was a shade paler, her eyes frightened.

"I found that bus ticket in your drawer a long time ago," I said. Then, because I suddenly knew it was true:

"You wanted to leave us. You were going to run away."

I expected her to slap me or strangle me or yell. Something. But she merely sat there while the air went slowly out of her. She sank against the cushions. She suddenly looked old to me.

"I didn't go," she said in a whispery voice. "I thought about it, I even bought the ticket, but..."

The air in the room became heavy—heavy enough to push me into the ground. I felt once again like a small child with short legs dangling over the edge of a chair. I had squandered my affection on this woman. I wanted to take back all those wasted kisses and dandelion bouquets. I wanted to pound bruises into her flesh. I wanted to cry. But I did none of these things. I looked straight at her and asked, "Why?"

Mom sighed. "Oh, Elise. I was so young when I married your dad. I was only a year older than you are now."

I tried to imagine myself as a bride in white satin, Miguel in a top hat and tuxedo. But no. We would be married differently, in the woods, perhaps. I could see myself garlanded with wildflowers, and he would somehow emerge from a veil-like mist on the back of a white stallion.

"Didn't you love Dad?"

Mom reached for my shoulder, but I twisted away. I wasn't about to let her soothe away her betrayal.

"Of course, honey," she said. "I still do. But don't you see? I went straight from daughter to wife. And then, before I could even catch my breath, I had babies. All of my dreams...poof! I felt like I was disappearing, too."

I didn't want to listen any longer. I couldn't forgive her in an afternoon. I got up and barricaded myself in my room. So what if she was sorry? So what if she had gotten over her restlessness and wanderlust? With her confession, she'd made my childhood a miserable lie.

She was a goddess fallen from grace. I wondered if Dad knew.

I vowed then and there that I would go through life without remorse. Madame Spencer had played an Edith Piaf song for us in class once, *"Rien de Rien."* It went through my head as I lay on the floor staring at the ceiling. *"Non, je ne regrette rien."* Her life had been full of hardships, but she wasn't sorry for anything. I would be like Edith Piaf or my great-grandmother, diving into shipwrecks and dashing off with her true love, not my mother, who stood over the kitchen sink daydreaming about her beauty queen days.

Meanwhile, I had more pressing concerns. My period was six weeks late.

19

After Chiara finished the rehab program at Timber Hills, she went back to boarding school. I imagined drab, sailor-collared uniforms and rows of beds like in the Madeline books. No wonder she had capitalized on her temporary freedom, I thought.

Although I was depressed on her behalf, Chiara's letters were full of her usual good cheer. She had started writing her novel and one of the characters was based on me. She had to keep her notebooks under her mattress so that they didn't fall into the wrong hands. I wasn't sure if she was worried about her fellow inmates or the iron-willed headmistress. At any rate, I imagined that all in-going mail was censored and I hesitated to write to her about my dilemma, though I badly needed her counsel. I finally decided to call her.

"The girls are having their study period now," a woman told me once I got through. Her British accent sounded fake.

"Please. I need to talk to her." I remembered one of Chiara's own ploys. "It's an emergency." I tried to lower my voice an octave, feigning middle age. "It's about her mother. There's been an accident."

"Oh, dear. I'll get her straight away."

I'd brought the phone into my room. The cord was

stretched taut. Even though I was alone, behind a closed door, I couldn't be sure of total privacy. I could hear Mom rattling pots in the kitchen, and Dad whistling over sports scores in the newspaper. Amanda was watching TV, and I could hear a commercial jingle touting toilet bowl cleaner. If I could hear them, they could probably hear me, too. I'd have to be careful.

"Hello?"

"Chiara! It's me, Elise. How are you?"

She burst out laughing. "You sly thang. Thanks for getting me out of there. It was deadly boring. So what's up in the land of the free?"

"Listen, I have a problem," I said. "Je suis enceinte."

Chiara gasped. "You're pregnant? Who's the daddy?"

"Remember the Gypsy musician in Chicago? That was Miguel. The carnie from last summer."

There was silence on the other end, and I pictured Chiara chewing on her lower lip, fitting the pieces into place. "Why didn't you tell me? Oh, well, never mind. Did you tell him?"

"That's the problem. I don't know where he is. He's been sending me these incredibly romantic letters from different towns, but there's no return address."

"What about your parents? Do they know?"

"Are you kidding? I'm hoping to prolong my life another month or two. At least until it's obvious." Honestly, I was terrified of telling my parents. My pregnancy would be the biggest scandal in the family since my great-grandmother, the flame-haired Margaret Stieg, in her fur coat and pearls, had hopped onto a train with her (alleged) bootlegger boyfriend, and disappeared out West, where there was hardly any water. Would my name be banned from conversation one day, too?

"You're going to keep it?"

"I don't know," I said. It occurred to me then that

Chiara couldn't help me. She didn't have any magic words, only questions. I would have to decide what to do on my own. An image of my pregnant mother jumping rope on the patio crept into my mind, but I shoved it away.

"You know, whatever you do, I'm behind you," Chiara said.

It sounded strange coming out of her mouth, like some phrase she'd picked up in group therapy, but I loved her for it. "I know you are," I said. "And thanks."

At school, I carried peppermint candies in my pockets to erase the taste of bile. I borrowed the hall pass in the middle of class so that I could vomit in private. The empty bathroom became my haven—a place for tears as well as sickness. The bulge in my belly was just barely noticeable, but I kept it hidden beneath billowy untucked men's shirts. As far as I could tell, no one had guessed my secret.

I went through the motions of school, homework, and watching TV, but my thoughts were held captive by a wandering man. His last letter, full of promises and passion, had been postmarked Bowling Green, Kentucky. That had been a month ago. There'd been nothing since.

I drew a red star on the map I kept under my bed. The stars were random, a crazy constellation revealing no clear path. I had no idea where he'd go next. And now I was trapped in daily desperation. Miguel's face had grown blurry in my mind, but I yearned for him still.

I didn't allow myself to consider the alternative—that I wouldn't find him, that I'd have to do everything on my own. I didn't ask myself the obvious questions: How would I support myself if I got thrown out of the house? What would my future hold? I guess I was living in a fairy tale.

In English class, we had to write a term paper. I chose the history of the Gypsies as my subject.

"Well, that's certainly original," Mrs. Caldwell, my English teacher said when I announced my topic. My classmates, in tune with current fads were writing about vampires and apartheid and punk rock. "What made you choose Gypsies?"

I looked her straight in the eye and said, "Fate." It sounded corny, but it was what I believed and I poured myself into this project with a sudden intensity. It was the only way I had of getting closer to Miguel. Plus, I thought I owed it to the baby growing inside of me to learn everything I could about its heritage.

When my child was old enough, I'd tell him, if it was a little coal-eyed boy, or her, if it was a little dancing girl, about the people who roamed the earth, starting in India and moving to the other countries of the world. I would tell that child about the thousands of Gypsies slaughtered by the Nazis in the Holocaust, about the persecution they endured even now. And although the Roma believed that outsiders—people like me—were dirty and impure, I would teach my child about the beauty of both cultures—mine and Miguel's. There were songs, stories, dances, and poems. These I would learn and teach to my baby.

The Gypsies were tribal, happiest in groups, and yet Miguel traveled alone. I wondered if he had been cast out for some reason. Maybe that was the reason for his pain. I had seen it in his gold-flecked eyes, heard it in the songs he played on his guitar.

I had to find him, be with him, assuage that awful loneliness. To hell with high school. Somehow I had to get to Miguel and tell him about our unborn child. We would be a family and give each other all the love we needed.

20

Valentine's Day. I decided upon February 14 as my deadline. Something, though I didn't know quite what, would happen by then. Miguel would show up on my doorstep, guitar in hand, words of love on his lips, waiting to take me away. Or he would call from a phone booth in Duluth, say, or Chattanooga, Tennessee. At the very least he would send me an address and free me from that awful stalemate. I was sick of waiting and I was beginning to show.

"So who are you going out with on Valentine's Day?" I asked my sister a week before.

Predictably, the romance with Lena hadn't lasted and Clark had promised half the galaxy to Amanda if she'd take him back. So far, she was having none of it. I admired her.

We were lying in our beds, murmuring in the dark as we sometimes did. Amanda rolled onto her side to face me. "I'm swearing off boys for a while," she said. "I'm going to devote myself to dance."

"No kidding?"

"Yeah. I want to get out of the corps. I want to be the principal ballerina for once."

I remembered Miss Burke, then, and the scandal that had driven her out of town years before. I know that

Amanda had been too young to understand why her starring role in The Nutcracker had been denied her, but I'd had a twinge of guilt when I'd heard that our former dance instructor was leaving Grand Haven. I never knew if it had been my fault. I don't think Mom had told anyone. Maybe someone else had caught Miss Burke and her lover in a reckless moment. At any rate, there wasn't much room in that town for those who lived by their own rules.

I thought about bringing all that up now, but I didn't. Amanda seemed so peaceful. She was being nice. "Hey, why don't we bake a cake for Valentine's Day? Remember how we used to do that?"

"Are you sure you should be eating cake, Miss Future Principal Ballerina?" I teased.

"We'll make it for Dad."

"Yeah, okay."

We lay there awhile longer. When at last her breaths had deepened, becoming soft purring snores, I got out of bed and went to the phone.

Mom and Dad were asleep, I guessed. I walked carefully, like a wildcat in the forest, avoiding the creaky floorboards as if they were snapping twigs. I barricaded myself in the bathroom with the phone and put towels along the cracks under the door to muffle sound. With a shaky finger, I dialed the first number.

The phone on the other end rang five times before someone picked it up. A gravelly voice called out "Grenoble's." Synthesized music and the clink of bottles were loud in the background.

"I'm trying to find someone. A musician who played at your club a few weeks ago." My heart was banging against my ribcage. I was sure the guy on the other end could hear the thunderous ker-thump, ker-thump.

"Say what?" the voice yelled. "I can hardly hear you.

Speak up."

"I'm looking for Miguel Ballersteros," I said loudly. "The Gypsy guitarist."

"Oh, yeah. Well, he ain't here. Sorry ma'am."

"Wait," I said. "Do you know where he went? On his tour, I mean. It's important that I find him. It's a family matter."

"I'd like to help you, lady, but I ain't his secretary and we're real busy right now."

It was often like that. After school, I pored over telephone directories at the public library, the one place I was allowed to go. At night, I furtively dialed the numbers I'd copied. Most of the time, my inquiries came to nothing, but once in a while I managed to find a cocktail waitress or a bartender or a rough-voiced bouncer who remembered him, who maybe had heard him play.

"I think he was going on to Charlotte," someone told me. The next day I pulled a thick Charlotte, North Carolina, phone book from the shelf and flipped to the yellow pages. I wrote down numbers for bars and nightclubs and coffee houses. I made my calls when the sky was black and the house quiet.

Sooner or later, a bill from Michigan Bell would arrive in our mailbox. With any luck, I'd be far away when that day came and wouldn't have to explain. At least not until later. I'd pay back every penny and apologize for every wrong thing I'd done, but first I had to take care of the bigger mess I'd gotten myself into.

The day before Valentine's Day, Amanda and I took over the kitchen and made a chocolate cake. I beat the eggs, my hand moving mechanically while my mind ran through a checklist. Clothes? Yes. I'd packed a small bag with enough to get me through a few weeks. It was warmer where I'd be going so I didn't need a lot. Plus, I was getting bigger by the day so most of my clothes were too tight. Zippers no longer meshed. Buttons popped off and rolled under furniture.

Money? I didn't have much of my own—only a few hundred dollars saved from babysitting and allowances, now tucked in among the billowy men's shirts I'd packed in a nylon duffel bag. As an emergency measure, I'd carefully ripped a blank check from the back of Mom's checkbook. She'd be mad when she found out, but think about all the money I'd save my parents by not going to college in the fall. Anyhow, I was only borrowing it. For a good cause.

"Uh, Elise," Amanda said. "I think you'd better stop beating now."

I yanked my thoughts back into the kitchen and grinned at her. Strands of brown hair had fallen out of her ponytail and into her eyes. There was a white fingerprint, like a chalk mark, on her cheek where she'd scratched. She stood beside me with a bowl of sifted flour and cocoa, waiting to mix in the liquid ingredients. The apron she wore over her Michigan State sweatshirt and corduroy jeans was frilly and oversized. On her, it looked like a costume.

I had a flashback to when we were both little girls, helping Mom make cookies. I remembered Amanda dipping her fingers into chocolate chip-studded dough and bringing globs to her mouth. That was back in the days when she'd looked at me with adoration, following my tracks like a duckling in its mother's wake. That was when Mom was our fairy princess and Dad had let us ride on his back while his necktie dragged on the floor. A sudden warmth washed over me. Nostalgia grabbed at my throat.

Lately, Amanda and I had grown closer. Without Clark, she was a different person and I liked her better. Only a few months before, the thought of the two of us baking a cake together would have been inconceivable. I realized that I would actually miss her. How strange it would be to lie down at night without her in the bed next to me. There would be none of the ritual murmurings that lulled us into sleep, no shared confidences, no silly squabbles.

Amanda must have seen the teardrop that trembled on my eyelash. My hormones had mutinied, and I found it impossible these days to control my emotions.

"What's wrong?" she asked, softly.

"Listen, Amanda. I'm going to tell you something, but you've got to promise you won't tell anyone. Especially Mom and Dad."

Her eyes widened and she set the bowl on the counter, ready to listen.

"I'm going away tomorrow," I said, lowering my voice to a whisper. "I have to find someone. I can't come back until I find him."

Amanda grabbed my arms. "What are you saying? You're running away? What about school?"

"School can wait. Amanda, I'm pregnant."

Her arms, suddenly drained of power, fell away. Her eyes on mine were full of horror, disbelief, and wonder. I knew she was thinking that girls like us, from good Christian middle-class families, didn't get pregnant. Or if they did, they took care of the problem before anyone knew. Only trashy girls became teen mothers. I read all this in my sister's eyes. Her gaze fell to that hard little mound under my baggy sweater.

"I—I knew you were gaining weight," she stammered, "but I never dreamed...."

As soon as she recovered, she'd be asking for details—who, when, where—but I wasn't going to tell. I was sure that Mom and Dad, if they knew, would do everything in their power to keep me away from my rambling man.

They'd probably put me in a home for unwed mothers and force me to put up my baby for adoption. If only I could find Miguel, everything would be all right.

The end of my trail was Columbia, South Carolina. This time the following day, I'd be on a bus bound for that land of ancient oaks and molasses vowels. I wouldn't come back till I found him.

I reached out to hug Amanda. "Remember. Don't tell anyone."

I could feel her nod against my shoulder. When we broke apart, I saw that she was crying, too.

21

The road rushed by underneath like a dark river. The pavement was illuminated by the spill of the bus's interior lights, but beyond was black. Once I saw two yellow eyes flash by—maybe a cat.

I was breathing a little easier since we'd crossed the state line, but I needed to put a few hundred more miles between me and Grand Haven before I'd feel relaxed enough to sleep. As it was now, Mom and Dad could still hop into their car and hope to catch up with me. The big Greyhound stopped off in every little town along the way. We'd even stopped at little country stores in the middle of nowhere. Every once in a while I looked behind us, expecting to see the headlights of Dad's station wagon. Every time I caught sight of a patrol car, my heart leapt into my throat.

Maybe I was paranoid, but I'd had a lot of time for thinking and imagining in the six hours since I'd boarded the bus. I went over the events leading up to my departure a million times, wondering if I'd left out the most important detail, or left behind a damning piece of evidence. I'd trashed the map beneath my bed. The pins had been extracted and the fifty states torn into confetti. Miguel's letters were bundled in ribbon and nestled in my bag, along with the check I'd forged and cashed. And even if Amanda couldn't keep her mouth shut, she wouldn't be able to tell anyone where I was going. I hadn't told her.

Valentine's Day had fallen on a Friday. Dad was planning on taking all of us out for dinner that night.

"Everyone will be jealous of me," he'd said, "dining with three beautiful women." It had been a long time since we'd all gone out to eat together.

Dad came home from work with roses for Mom.

"They're gorgeous," she said, before smacking him on the lips.

He plucked two blossoms and handed one to Amanda and one to me. "Happy Valentine's Day, girls."

I felt a pang. When Dad found out about my predicament, he'd be heartbroken. Just thinking about his reaction brought tears to my eyes. I was used to the Wrath of Mom, but Dad's wounded silences were another matter. I hoped someday I'd have a chance to make up for the damage I'd done, that I was going to do.

"Are you ladies ready to go to the Bilmar?" He'd booked us a table at a restaurant on the beach.

In truth, I'd liked to have gone. It would be nice to feast on steak with my family around me and the sound of the surf in my ears. I bit my lip to keep from crying. Lately, I was always on the verge of tears. It was the hormones, I guess.

"Dad, I don't feel so well. I'll stay home."

His face dimmed and his eyebrows furrowed in concern.

"Oh, honey. Not tonight," Mom said. She pressed a palm to my forehead. "You don't seem to be running a fever, but if you feel bad we can wait till tomorrow night. I'd hate to leave you behind, especially when you're sick."

If she only knew…

Mom was dressed up, her makeup freshly applied. It

wouldn't take much to push her out the door to her long-awaited night on the town.

"No, please. Go on ahead. I'll be fine."

"Are you sure?"

"Positive. I'll have a pot pie out of the freezer and go to bed."

Mom patted my cheek doubtfully. She seemed to be searching my face for symptoms, or maybe for permission. Finally, she kissed my temple and stepped toward the door.

I listened to the roar of the engine in the driveway and then to its fading. The house suddenly seemed quieter than it had ever been. The clock on the kitchen wall ticked loudly, reminding me that I didn't have a lot of time. The bus station was three miles away, and I was walking.

When I sauntered into Larry's Dairy Bar an hour later, I felt like a prisoner crossing into freedom. This is what it was like to clear the Berlin Wall, I thought. I ordered an ice cream cone to celebrate.

"Where you headed to, young lady?" The man behind the counter nodded at the ticket I held in one hand.

"New York City," I lied. I wasn't going to make it easy for anyone to find me. "I'm going to visit my grandmother."

"That's nice." He ran a damp cloth over the counter. "There's a lot to do in New York. You going to go see a play on Broadway?"

"Maybe." I swiped my tongue at a drip of mint chocolate chip.

The glass window over the ice cream bins trembled as a bus pulled up in front of the shop. It wheezed to a stop and spat out a middle-aged woman in a fur-collared coat. My chariot had arrived.

I nodded at the guy who'd scooped my ice cream.

"See ya." I faked a cool that I didn't feel. My head was as light as a helium-filled balloon.

"Give my regards to Greta Garbo," he said.

The bus was only half full. I took a seat near the back and dropped my bag on the floor. "Let's go, let's go," I prayed. When the bus started to move, I'd whispered, "Thank you."

I must have dozed off because the next thing I knew, morning rays were warming my cheek and all the license plates said Kentucky. I looked out at emerald fields and grazing horses, their russet hides gleaming in the sun. The expansive terrain calmed me. I could breathe easier now.

The money from the check I'd forged would last me a few months if I was careful. Careful meant a room at the Y.W.C.A., instant noodles in a cup, walking instead of riding. After thirty-six hours on a bus, breathing in my own sour scent and banging my head against the window in sleep, "careful" was enough to make me weep. I hadn't slept well, waking at every stop along the way. My bowels were clogged with half a dozen starchy diner meals. For just one night I would pamper myself.

I dragged my duffel bag out of the terminal and to the curb. I couldn't see much of the city. It was getting dark, after all, and the bus station wasn't exactly centrally located. There were train tracks up the hill, like a zipper cutting through land. I saw a yard full of junky cars—smashed up metal, doorless sedans. Where were the magnolia trees, the fried chicken stands, my *Gone with the Wind* South?

I climbed into a cab. The driver was chewing a matchstick. His skin was brown, but the whites of his eyes were as pure as new snow.

"Where to?" he asked, the match bobbing in his

mouth.

"The Holiday Inn." I figured there had to be one nearby. After all, this was America.

"The one downtown?"

"Yes."

He didn't say any more. I was glad because I wanted to watch out the window and I was tired of talking to strangers.

We drove down a street lined with brick houses. Their small yards were patchy, stomped upon. I saw a cluster of young people in one yard. They were holding plastic cups and a blast of music hit us as we went by. A party. They were probably college students.

There was the life I would have led—flirting and drinking and listening to music. My friends and I would talk about Baudelaire and Georgia O'Keefe and R.E.M. We'd make love with brainy boys on futons, in moonlit parks, in abandoned buildings. Part of me wanted this life, a skein of endless possibilities. Another part of me, the part that had brought me to this unknown city, yearned for a blurry-faced man with magic fingers. I thought I'd die if I didn't find him.

We cruised down a street festooned with traffic signals, past a great domed building surrounded by a lawn with towering trees, benches, and bronze men on horses. From the peak of this building, three flags waved—the Stars and Stripes, the flag of the Confederacy, and another one emblazoned with a palmetto tree.

We turned a corner. The driver stopped and asked for five dollars.

At the front desk, I paid in cash. I thought a minute before registering, and then wrote "Lena Groves." I was undercover. The sense of intrigue enlivened me, gave me enough energy to make it to my room, into the tub, and into bed. Sleep was sudden and heavy. Nothing woke me for the next fourteen hours.

My first impulse the next morning was to order room service. A plate of scrambled eggs and jellied toast would barely dent my wad, I told myself. But then the responsible angel on my other shoulder whispered, "Remember what you're here for."

Where to look? And when? Night seemed like a good time. He would be near music.

I washed my face with the little bar of hotel soap, put on clean clothes, and washed the ones I'd worn the day before in the sink. When they were hung and dripping from the shower rod, I grabbed my key and left the room.

I'd slept past the morning check-out time, but that was okay. I could afford one more night. It would give me a little time to find somewhere else to stay.

The clerk at the front desk told me I could get breakfast at the Capital Café.

The diner was easy to find, and not too busy midmorning. A few people of retirement age sat on counter stools, slurping coffee and reading *The State* newspaper. I tried to peer over a flannel-shirted shoulder. Was there a picture of me? A story about a missing girl? No, nothing. I was both disappointed and relieved.

I slouched into a booth near the jukebox. A waitress came over. Her name tag said, "Pee Wee," and though she was small in stature, her tight-lipped glare said, "Don't mess with me."

"What you want?" And what of that famed Southern hospitality?

I ordered a grilled cheese sandwich, a glass of milk, and salad. I was thinking calcium, vitamins. I had to think about the baby.

Pee Wee came back a little while later carrying everything balanced on one arm. She was smiling—the residue of a laugh. Maybe the cook had just told her a joke. At any rate, she wasn't so scary anymore.

"Have you ever heard of a place called Rockafella's?" I asked. Miguel had played there on Acoustic Night a week or so ago.

"Down in Five Points," Pee Wee said.

"Five Points?" I raised my eyebrows. "Sorry, I'm from out of town."

She pointed east. I didn't figure she'd draw me a map. Well, I had all day to find it.

22

I could have gotten in if I'd really wanted to. I still had the fake ID that had been my passport into those Chicago clubs. And the weight I'd put on, the bags under my eyes, made me look far older than eighteen. Probably no one would card me at all.

I decided to stay outside. I lingered in the shadows and watched people line up. Clean-cut boys in Oxford shirts flashed their driver's licenses and slipped inside. A bevy of big-haired girls flirted with the bouncer and got in without paying the cover charge. There were all kinds—frou frou debutantes, tattooed rednecks, vampire-types with pale skin and crow-black clothes—but no Miguel.

During a lull in traffic, the bouncer turned to me and said, "Can I help you?"

I jumped. I'd thought I was invisible. I ran a hand through my hair, trying to appear casual. "Well, yes. Maybe. See, I'm trying to find someone—a guitarist who played here a couple weeks ago. I was thinking he might still be around." My voice faded into the night. He probably thought I was some groupie. "It's a family matter," I quickly added.

The scraggly-haired man didn't blink twice. He'd probably heard stranger things. He rubbed a hand over chin stubble and began to nod. "Yeah, Miguel. I remember him. Spanish guy, right?"

"Roma," I corrected. "He's a Gypsy. Do you know where he is?"

"Can't say that I do. He's been back a few times since he played here, but I haven't seen him tonight. If he comes in, I could tell him you're looking for him. What's your name?"

I told him.

The next morning, I checked into the Dixieland Motel. At only twenty dollars a night, it was a bargain compared to the Holiday Inn. Plus, it was a short stroll from Five Points, which is where I decided I needed to be. If Miguel was anywhere in the city, it was there, where the young congregated in open air cafes in the afternoons and scouted the streets at night, looking for a party or a good band. That evening and every evening after, I was looking, too.

Chiara had already shown me how music could charm. I'd fallen under its spell in a dark basement a thousand miles away. It was no surprise then to feel myself pulled by a voice to the door of Rockafella's.

I'd been spying for seven nights by then, lurking in the shadows, or staked out at a fast food restaurant on the edge of the parking lot. I'd nurse a Coke or an unsweetened iced tea for an hour while I studied every person who walked by the window.

On this particular night, the beat of the drums had gotten under my skin and the jangly guitars seemed to be calling my name. The marquis indicated that a group called The Glass Bead Game was on stage. I recognized the name in a vague sort of way—something spotted once on a library shelf. It struck me as mystical and magical, and I was deeply intrigued.

So the name and the music drew me, and something else as well. I was lonely. I wanted to brush up against those people I'd seen streaming into the club each night. Some of the faces were familiar to me by now. I'd gotten used to the thin, carrot-topped guy who always wore a loose tweed coat and round, tinted glasses. And then there was a young woman whose heavy eye makeup was visible from a hundred yards away. Every night she dressed in a black outfit that matched her fuzzy hair.

I went up to the door and handed over a crumpled five-dollar bill and my fake ID. The bouncer beamed a flashlight onto my laminated photo, glanced at my face, and stamped my hand with red ink. I'd never gone into a bar alone before, and I felt awkward. What to do with my arms? How should I stand? Everyone in the smoky chamber seemed to know each other. Small groups huddled and clinked beer bottles together. Up toward the stage, heads bobbed up and down in time to the beat. A few people slammed from side to side, laughing when they got knocked to the floor.

I climbed on a stool and ordered a Coke. I needed something in my hands.

I'd only been sitting there for a few minutes when a pimply-faced guy with a blond crew cut sidled up to me. "Hey, good-lookin'. Can I buy you a drink?"

I raised my Coke in mute response, but he didn't give up. "Do you go to college here?"

I shook my head, then just to be polite, asked, "Do you?"

"No, ma'am. I'm stationed at Fort Jackson. C'ant you tell by my haircut?" He rubbed the top of his freshly shorn head and I smiled.

Encouraged, he went on. "Hey, do you like this music?"

I nodded. My foot had begun tapping of its own

accord.

He leaned closer as if he were about to tell me a secret. "Did you know that the singer is a witch?"

I raised my eyebrows.

"That's what people say."

The band onstage was long-haired and hippie-looking. The men wore frayed bell-bottoms while the woman at the mike floated about in a flowered granny dress.

I listened to the soldier-in-training drone on while I searched the place. I caught sight of the redhead. He'd taken off his coat and glasses. When the light flashed his way, I caught a glimpse of iridescence painted on his eyelids. I'd never seen a man in makeup before, but he looked good. Having spotted him, I felt less lonely.

I turned back to my suitor. He was talking about hunting. I decided it was time to escape. "Could you excuse me for just a minute?" I asked sweetly. "I need to go to the restroom."

Something in his basset hound eyes told me he'd heard that line before, but I headed to the back of the club and joined the waiting women. A sudden weariness overcame me. I leaned against the wall and closed my eyes. Two women were talking.

"Hey, Maggie, where's that roommate of yours?"

"Dean? You mean you haven't heard? He's taken off to follow the Grateful Dead."

"Really? So you're living alone now?"

"Actually, Miguel's staying with me. Remember him? That Gypsy? But I don't think he has enough to pay this month's rent."

My eyes snapped open. I found myself looking straight at Maggie, the frizzy-haired woman in black. My mouth fell open while I tried to think of something to say. Just then, the girl behind me nudged my back. "It's your turn." I nodded dumbly, and pushed open the bathroom door.

Part of me was afraid that Maggie would evaporate into thin air in the time it took me to hoist up my dress. Another part feared that I'd imagined the whole thing, that Maggie had been born of my strong wish. I flushed and washed my hands and could have hugged that dark-eyed woman with her halo of frizz when I found her still there. She was shifting from foot to foot as if the pressure on her bladder was getting to her, so I thought it best to wait. She went into the bathroom. When she came back out, I grabbed her arm.

"Yes?"

"I-I couldn't help overhearing you a little earlier," I stammered. "You were talking about Miguel?"

"Yeah? What about him?" The music, her friends, the beer—they were all calling to her, and I knew my hold on her attention was fragile at best. I plunged right in.

"I've been looking for him. I'm pregnant and he's my friend and I really need to talk to him."

Her eyes got bigger. For such a jaded-looking girl, she seemed surprised by my outburst.

"I don't mean to sound like a lunatic," I said, releasing her arm, "and if you and Miguel are having a...a relationship, I'm sorry. I just need to see him once."

Maggie looked tough, but I figure she had a tender heart because she agreed to take me home. We walked through Five Points, past darkened shops and drunken revelers.

"I have to tell you, Elise, that he isn't well." That's all she had to say about him. She told me a little about her money problems and said I could stay with her if I helped out with the rent. I was looking forward to checking out of the Dixieland Motel.

Finally, Maggie led me up a hill onto a residential street. The house looked shabby even in the dark. The porch sagged and creaked when we stepped onto it. Paint was flaking off the door.

I didn't notice the house much as she led me to Miguel's room. My mind was too busy working out what I would say. Should I be coy? "So, did you miss me?" Should I fly into his arms? Cover him with kisses? Maggie knocked on a closed door off the living room. She pressed her ear against the wood. Apparently, she heard a reply, because she pushed her way in. I followed.

There was a mattress against the wall opposite me, and there was a man lying on the mattress, but I didn't recognize him right away. This man was gaunt, his long black hair dull and limp. His eyes were closed and he didn't move. For a moment, I thought he might be dead and a shiver rippled down my spine.

"Okay if I turn on the light?" Maggie was already reaching for the switch.

I looked around, hoping for some clue to help me get my bearings. The room was furnished with only the mattress and a straight-backed chair that might have been pulled from some junk pile. A moth fluttered against the naked bulb. Clothes were tossed in the corner, and two full ashtrays were placed on the floor, ready to spill at any moment. There was no guitar. Maybe this wasn't the right Miguel after all.

Then he opened his eyes and I saw that it was. He didn't seem surprised to see me, only tired. He was as pale as the moon. I wondered about what Maggie had said. Was he sick? Starving?

He slowly rose and came to me. Maggie eased herself out of the room, leaving us alone. He reached for my hands and held them like reins, that mound of baby between us.

I felt a kick and my hand went to my belly. It was almost as if Miguel's weight and vigor had been transferred to the child inside of me.

"Elise," Miguel said. His voice had not changed. I closed my eyes for a moment and was sucked back into the past, to the day I first met him.

"She's getting big, isn't she?"

I opened my eyes just as he released my hands and put his on my belly.

"How do you know it's a girl?"

"I know," he said, quietly.

I wondered if his mother had told him about that, too.

I waited for him to embrace me, but after a moment, his hands fell away. "Come on," he said. "Let's go for a walk."

My ankles were swollen and I was bone-tired, but I nodded.

Out on the sidewalk, we strolled under stars, hands brushing from time to time.

"I told you we'd be together again," Miguel said.

"Then why didn't you come to me? And if you knew I was pregnant, why didn't you try to help me?"

He shrugged. "I knew you would come."

"What's next?" I said. "What do we do now?"

He said nothing, kept walking, spine bent toward the earth. I was afraid of his sorrow, afraid that it meant something bad would happen to my unborn child.

"I'm going to have this baby," I said. "I'm not going to give it up."

"No," he said flatly. "I don't expect you to."

"Even if I have to raise it on my own, even if you don't want to have anything to do with us..." And then I was sobbing. It was the hormones, I told myself. The hormones, the bus trip, my breaking heart. Had I really been so stupid as to imagine he'd marry me? That we'd go from town to town, traveling through carnivals and bars, living that Gypsy life together? Or that we'd journey in caravans across Europe, camping among the wild white horses of Camargue, the staccato-stepping flamenco dancers of Spain, all those places Chiara had told me about?

Miguel paused under a streetlight and pulled a clean bandana from his jeans pocket. He dabbed at my tears and then finally pulled me into his arms.

"It's just that I love you," I said.

"Shhh. I know."

When we went back to his room, I laid down with him on his mattress. After he went to sleep, I crept out of the room and went outside to sit on the porch. Maggie came out a little while later and sat down beside me.

"So where did you come from, anyhow?" she asked.

I told her.

She shook her head and whistled. "All that way on a bus, just to see Miguel."

"His mother was a fortune teller," I said. "She saw me in his future."

Maggie snorted. "I don't believe I've ever met anyone as dumb as you." She must have seen the look on my face because she looped an arm around my shoulder. When she spoke again, her voice was soft. "When I met Miguel, he told me that same thing. And then he asked for fifty bucks."

It was a warm night, and the moon was bright and friendly overhead, but I felt a chill creeping through my body. It started in my feet and rose upward till I felt ice around my heart.

Maggie stared down the street, letting me absorb this shock in silence. Although the wrinkles raying from her eyes and the dull cast of her skin told of experience and hard living, I knew there must have been a time when she'd read fairytales and believed every word. Once, she must have found rolling down a grassy hill the purest pleasure. Maybe I would be like Maggie in a few years—bitter, used up, sick of the world. I shuddered.

Maggie felt it and held me closer. Finally, she looked at my belly. "Is it his? Is that why you came all this way?"

I nodded, unable to speak. My throat was jammed with held-back sobs.

"Damn." Maggie shook her head again. She looked as sad as I felt. "You saw him. He's not going to make much of a father. What are you gonna do?"

I'll save him, I thought, though I didn't know how. Part of me believed that love was a serum I could spoon into his mouth. It would nourish his soul and make a happy ending.

"Do you have any money?" Maggie asked.

I wasn't about to tell her how much I'd brought. She might try to make me hand all of it over for room and board or some personal emergency. My instincts told me to be discreet. "A little," I said. "Enough to get by."

"Well, like I said. You're welcome to stay here for as long as you need. You can sleep on the couch if you like."

She led me back into the living room, to a burgundy crushed velvet sofa I'd failed to notice earlier.

I couldn't help but think of my mother. At this point, she would have presented a guest with a stack of neatly folded bed linens and towels, and a nice, soft pillow. Maggie, however, didn't seem to notice my reluctance to lie down. The material was matted in some places as if someone had spilled syrup on the upholstery. Random cigarette burns dotted the fabric, and the back of the sofa was slightly gray as if it had absorbed the grease of unwashed hair. Chiara's voice came into my head: "Oh, Elise. You're so bourgeois!"

I sighed deeply. She was right. I would have much preferred the starched white sheets of the Holiday Inn or my own bed, next to Amanda's, back in Michigan. But I'd come this far, too far to erase everything that had happened and go back to the way I was. All right. I'd sleep on that ratty sofa. At least it would be better than the Dixieland Motel. And Miguel, for what it was worth, was nearby.

"Could I have a sheet or something?" I asked.

Maggie laughed. "Sorry. I've only got one set and it's on my bed right now." She went into her room then, closing the door behind her.

I stretched out along the length of the sofa and tried to ignore its stale smells. At least it was soft. At least there were no bedsprings creaking on the other side of the wall.

My sleep that night was hard-won. I woke to every sound—the passage of a train through town, the scratch of mouse feet on the kitchen linoleum. Another time, toward morning, I felt a tickle on my chin as if silk threads were trailing over my face. My eyes opened to a figure bending over me, knuckles gently brushing my cheek. "Shh. Sleep, Elise. My angel girl." I closed my eyes again, knowing that I was exactly where I was supposed to be.

The next thing I knew, I was alone in the house. I glanced around the room, looking for a note, some indication of where everyone had gone off to and when they were coming back, but of course there was none. I was not an honored guest. I splashed some water on my face. The bathroom sink was iron stained and bore traces of scum. The shower curtain was dappled with mildew. Housework was obviously low priority here, but such squalor made my skin crawl.

Outside, the sun was high above. The fresh air was delicious and invigorating after all those hours inside. I decided to walk a few blocks to the Eckerd's I'd seen the day before and pick up some cleaning supplies. I'd earn my keep. It didn't look like there was anything in that house worth stealing, so I didn't worry about locking it.

My money—all that I had left—was rolled into a tight wad and tucked into my bra. I peeled off a twenty and stuck it into my wallet, and then I wandered down the slight incline to the store. I loaded up a basket with as much as I could carry—sponges, powdered cleanser, toilet bowl cleaner, some hard bristly brushes, and rubber gloves. Then I climbed back up the hill and got to work.

When Maggie burst through the door later that evening, I was resting on the sofa with my feet propped up. She stood in the doorway and sniffed. "What's that smell?"

"Pine Sol. I cleaned the house."

She scowled. "Why?"

"Because it was dirty."

"I hope you didn't go into my room."

"Of course not." She could have said "thank you" or "you shouldn't have" or "bless your little heart." I hadn't expected scorn. Well, at least I was happier. I was no longer scratching at imaginary creepy crawlies.

Maggie didn't say anything else. She threw down the paper bag she was carrying and stomped into the kitchen. I could hear her yanking open cupboard doors and sorting through the pans.

I sighed. In a little while, there would be dirty dishes in that pristine sink—bowls stuck with bits of dried noodles. Exhaustion washed over me like a slow wave. I pillowed my head with a clean rolled-up towel and fell asleep.

23

I was learning how to cook. By the first day of spring, I'd mastered grilled cheese sandwiches and canned soup. My tuna salad wasn't bad either. Now, I was working on a spaghetti sauce. There wasn't a cookbook in the house, and the other two residents were short of culinary skills, so I was just winging it.

Cooking gave me something to do while Maggie was off waiting tables at Yesterday's in Five Points and Miguel was out wandering the streets. When he came back, I'd set a bowl of canned chili or a charred pork chop in front of him. He always smiled and kissed my cheek and ate a few bites, but he kept getting thinner and thinner. It was as if his pounds were magically grafting onto my body.

I had an appetite that wouldn't quit. I spent my precious dollars on healthy vegetables and lean meats—enough for both Miguel and me—but after I finished a meal, the baby cried out for huge globs of chocolate ice cream, French fries, and apple pie. More than once, I found myself headed for the Tastee Freeze.

I tried to take care of Miguel. I washed his clothes, hung his blankets out on the rickety porch railing to air, and made his meals. But the sadness that had settled over him would not go away.

When he had come to me two days after my arrival

and kissed me long and hard, I had forgotten about music. More important, I thought, was the warm flesh that I pressed against and the musky, smoky scent of him. We lay on his makeshift bed for hours, it seemed, kissing and caressing—only that. Then I held him as he lapsed into sleep and wondered what would happen next.

Now, remembering, I couldn't believe I'd been so dense.

"Miguel," I said, across our bowls of chicken noodle soup. "Would you play me a song on your guitar after lunch? A Gypsy song?"

He stared into the golden broth for a long moment. "The guitar is gone," he said.

"What?"

"I pawned it. I ran out of money."

We both fell into silence. I watched Miguel dip his spoon into his soup. There was finally something I could do for him, something that would surely chase away his demons. I would find his guitar and buy it back.

Miguel left the house after lunch as he always did. I never asked where he went. I figured he had a nomadic need, a predisposition to wander. I let him go each day, knowing he would eventually return.

I gave him a head start before I took off. I'd come across a cluster of pawn shops in my early explorations of the city, up the street from the Holiday Inn.

The weather had cooled off some. I put one of Miguel's dark jackets over my floaty dress. Nothing matched. I was dressed as haphazardly as the bums I saw digging through garbage cans.

I walked through Five Points, over the railroad tracks, past the houses of college students, beyond the campus with its well-groomed lawns, and past the café where I'd had my first breakfast in Columbia. My feet were tired by the time I made it to Assembly Street. I was tempted to plop down on the sidewalk to rest, but my mother's voice floated into my head: "It wouldn't look right." That moment, I was too worn out to argue with her, so I kept going.

When I reached the first pawn shop, I didn't go in, but studied the window display until I'd memorized it. An array of diamond rings sparkled in the sunlight, making me think of bad luck and broken hearts. Watches ticked, knives glinted, and a few musical instruments hung in silent suspension. I spotted a saxophone and a violin, but no guitar. I went on to the next shop.

My hope was dimming. Nothing in the three shops I visited resembled what I was looking for. What if someone had bought it? I was just about to drag myself back across town when my eyes fell upon a music store two doors down. It wasn't a pawn shop, per se, but maybe they had some used goods in stock.

I marched right in and there it was—Miguel's guitar with its wood the color of Kentucky horses' hides. It was off to one side, propped up on velvet, flanked by a somewhat battered trumpet and a clarinet. I wrapped my fingers around its neck, making my claim, and took it to the cash register.

I must have looked like a street musician carrying that thing downtown. Perhaps those who paid any attention expected me to throw down a hat and start a song. If only I could, I thought. Then I wouldn't have to worry about my dwindling funds. Well, maybe this guitar would save its rightful owner. I couldn't wait to return it to him.

He found it soon enough, leaning against his bed with a red ribbon around its neck. He brought it into the living room where I was resting and said, "Where'd you get this?"

"I thought you'd feel better if you started playing

again."

He stared at me as if I was speaking another language. I tried to explain more. "Miguel, you're so talented. You could cut a record. You could be famous like..." and here, thanks to Chiara and Matt, a name jumped into my mouth "...Django Rheinhardt."

Miguel slowly shook his head and let the guitar slip from his grasp. The strings sounded a muffled protest.

"No, you don't understand. I will never be a famous musician."

I started to argue, but he held up his hand. What he said next sent a chill up and down my spine.

"I have no future. I have reached the end of what was predicted for me."

A girl with grain-gold hair, I thought. Eyes the color of a lake in summer. Was my entrance, then, the cue for his exit? But no, I didn't believe in all that—tarot cards, tea leaves, palmed destinies. And yet, a Gypsy woman's words had persuaded me to get on a bus and cross the country.

It occurred to me that sometimes people need stories to help themselves get through the hard parts of life. Just as Mom had told us stories about tap dancing in Mexico, just as I had filled nights with mermaid tales, maybe Miguel's mother had told him stories to pull him through an unhappy boyhood. Now there were no more stories left and no one to tell them. Except for me.

I reached over and picked up his hand. He didn't resist when I uncurled his fingers one by one and bent over his exposed palm. With one finger, I traced the lines that rivered his skin. My own palms were marked by three long intersecting creases, but Miguel's wrinkles seemed random, broken. I stroked my fingertip across the base of his thumb and said, "You will become the father of a bright, bouncy baby. You will have love and laughter and peace of mind."

But he didn't warm to my vision. He snatched his hand away and balled it up again.

I didn't know what else I could do.

24

"I can't understand why y'all are so gloomy," Maggie said. She'd just breezed in from Yesterday's and was standing in the middle of the living room, unbuttoning her blouse. She had no modesty and didn't care if the neighbors across the street got a free strip show.

"If anyone's got a right to be down in the dumps, it's me," she went on.

I'd heard all this before, but I figured I'd let her go through it again. Maybe it was like therapy for her. I watched as she pawed through a heap of freshly washed clothes, looking for something black. She found a T-shirt and yanked it over her head.

"You know, my mama was murdered when I wasn't but fourteen years old." Maggie smoothed the shirt over her flat stomach and went into her room to grab a handful of clunky jewelry. "And my stepmother, the old hag, tried to put me away in the loony bin."

I always listened, but I wasn't sure how much of her story was true. Maggie did, after all, have a tendency to stick little pieces of paper under her tongue and start hallucinating. Once she'd seen monkeys swinging from the light fixture. All I knew for certain was that she had thick welts down her wrists. They were lengthwise, not crosswise, as if she'd really wanted to die.

"Hey, why don't you come out with me tonight?" She was in front of me now, eyes all smudged with kohl. "It would do you good."

I had to agree that anything was better than sitting there all night, wondering about Miguel. I didn't know where he was, only that he'd gone out wandering again.

"All right," I said. "But I feel dumpy."

"Don't say that. You look good, like Little Miss Mother Nature herself." She lent me a string of glass beads and spritzed me with cologne. I still felt dumpy, but I appreciated her attention.

"Do you want to drop some acid?" she asked.

I saw that she was about to put one of those little paper scraps in her mouth. I just looked at her at first. "No. I can't."

"Why not?"

"You know," I said, patting my stomach. "The baby."

I knew that I was supposed to be going to a doctor and getting prenatal care, but I couldn't drag myself to a clinic. I was worried I'd be arrested for running away and sent back to my parents. I still had this nutty idea that, with patience, everything would work itself out. Eventually, Miguel would start to love the little being that swam in my womb. Then we'd get jobs, get married, and sing along to Miguel's guitar.

Maggie and I walked to Rockafella's. Some of her friends had formed a new band and they were making their debut. They hadn't started playing yet. The bartender was spinning vinyl on a sound system behind the bar.

Maggie sang along, a song about wanting to be tied to the back of someone's car.

Without a big name headliner to draw people in, the crowd was sparse. Only the diehard regulars had gathered.

I sat down on a stool and asked for water. Maggie began mingling with her friends. I saw the guy with red hair come in through the door. He was wearing the round tinted glasses and that big tweed coat. The familiarity of him warmed me. When Maggie came by to check on me, I asked her who he was.

"That's Noel," she said. "He's in tonight's band. Wanna meet him?"

"Maybe later." I felt large and lumpy, in no state for meeting alluring young men. I only wanted to watch this one and admire the way he glided across the floor.

At last the band members began to arrange and adjust their instruments and equipment. A guy with dark curly hair and round glasses like Noel's angled the mike toward his mouth and said, "How y'all doing tonight?"

A feeble cheer went up.

"We're Congaree Cur. This is our first gig, and I'm real glad y'all came out to hear us...."

He went on for a while, but I had stopped listening. My attention was fixed on the guitar that Noel had strapped over his shoulder. I'd first seen it in Chicago, and later I'd bought it and carried it across town on blistered feet. It hadn't been played since I'd brought it to Miguel, but somehow I'd believed it was still there, tucked away in a closet for safekeeping. Now this.

My first impulse was to run out of there and start bawling. There were a million things to mourn—Miguel's hope, the loss of his music, and my thirty dollars, among them. Fear tightened on my heart like a vise. I had endowed that guitar with magical healing properties, but now I could see that I'd been wrong. It was simply wire and wood.

I forced myself to stay and listen. The sounds that Noel coaxed from those strings were different from Miguel's, but soothing all the same. The band had a bluesy sound, but there was hope underneath. And though some of the melodies were sad, the audience did not cry and wring their hands. They danced.

I went home before Maggie. She was with a new man, on the verge of romance. I'd be in the way of sweet talk if I stayed. Plus, I was tired.

I was dreaming meadows. Buttercups, daisies, timothy weed. And then a lake, roiling waves, me in a rocky rowboat.

"Elise, you'd better wake up. There's been an accident."

As I swam up from the depths of slumber, I realized that the rocking wasn't from water, but Maggie's hands. She rolled me from side to side. Her words, when they registered, reminded me of Chiara. Was this another of her jokes? A way out of class? Nothing truly bad ever happened, did it? But when I was fully awake, something about Maggie's wild eyes made me afraid.

"What?"

"It's Miguel. He's done gone and got himself run over by a train."

Her words were a vacuum, sucking every other thought out of my head. Finally, I whispered, "Is he dead?"

She nodded. "He's in pieces. Like Humpty Dumpty." She started laughing, all weird and hysterical. Maybe it was the acid. Maybe he wasn't really dead.

I got out of bed and grabbed the nearest shirt and leggings. I didn't bother brushing my hair. It didn't matter much what I looked like.

Maggie led the way out into the dark, down the hill. We went through the business district of Five Points, past the art galleries, the used record store and incense vendors, and up the next incline. There was quite a crowd for such an hour. A few drunken frat boys who'd witnessed the accident on their way home were giving statements to the police. A woman in robe and curlers and a couple of winos lingered on the perimeter. An ambulance had arrived. Too late for that, I thought. White-smocked attendants were combing the overgrown grasses along the tracks. I didn't want to think about what they were looking for.

I stood in the middle of the clamor, frozen, oblivious. I didn't notice the cop standing nearby till he was right in front of me. He held a plastic bag filled with scraps of fabric.

"Excuse me, ma'am," he said softly.

I looked into his young, sad face. He seemed fresh out of the police academy, not yet jaded by the misfortunes of others. "Are you by any chance Elise Faulkner?"

I stared blankly, not quite appreciating his prescience. "Yes. How did you know?"

He fished a hand into the plastic bag and pulled out a laminated card. "This was in one of the deceased's pockets."

I hadn't seen my driver's license since Chicago. Miguel had no use for such a thing, and yet he'd carried it with him everywhere. He had died with my face in his pocket.

I began to cry then. My howls echoed through Five Points and were answered by neighboring dogs. No one could console me—not the young, kind policeman, nor his older gray-haired partner, nor Maggie, who was quite undone herself. Only the needle that went into my arm in the back of the ambulance could stop those screams.

25

Through the first few weeks of grieving, I slept in Miguel's bed and wore his clothes—at least the ones that fit. His other possessions had been flown back to his Gypsy mother, along with his remains. I had been surprised to find that she was still alive and that Miguel had been writing to her all this time. I thought of writing to her myself, telling her about her grandchild, maybe appealing for help. But something about her frightened me. I pictured a woman with a scarf over her head, seated behind a crystal ball, dealing out doom. I did not want to live under her knowing eyes and I blamed her for Miguel's death.

He had left me nothing—no good-bye letter, no photograph—and although it wasn't money or material I wanted, I craved a souvenir. I thought of the guitar.

Maggie told me that Noel worked in the rare book room at the university library. I decided to pay him a visit, maybe work out a deal. I was ready to prostrate myself, beg if I had to.

I found him sequestered on the third floor. He was alone in a wide, hushed hall, seated at a desk. At his left, was the door to the cool chamber where the fragile pages of dead masters were kept. The dark paneling, the dim lighting, made me think I was in a basement. There was no picture window overlooking the reflecting pool outside, no glimpse of waving palmettos or shivering oak leaves.

Noel's coppery head was bent over this work when I walked in the door. In his mossy cardigan, he looked like a librarian, but then his head jerked up and I saw lilac-dusted eyelids. At first, he looked wary, caught, but then his pale features gave way to surprise and a smile. Without the round glasses, he seemed closer somehow, less intimidating.

"I hope I'm not bothering you," I said.

"No, not at all." He came out from behind the desk as if he were about to pull out a chair for me but there wasn't any furniture for guests. "I was in the middle of typing up file cards for Beatrix Potter books and bored to tears. I'm glad you came."

I thought it was an odd thing to say since we'd never met. "I'm Elise," I said.

"I know. You live with Maggie, right?"

I nodded. So they'd talked about me. A rush of pleasure filled my chest.

"I was wondering if I might be able to persuade you to sell your guitar. I was close to Miguel and I'd like to have a memento."

Noel's eyes slid over my face. He bit his lip while he chose his words. "I will," he began slowly, "under one condition."

My heart sank. "What's that?"

"If you'll join me for a cup of coffee."

I blushed. Even my ears warmed up. When I spoke again, my voice was tiny. "I'm not in any condition to start something."

He smiled. "Just a cup of coffee."

We wandered over to the student concessionaire at the Russell House and ordered drinks. The beautiful late spring weather lured us back out of doors to a plush lawn and the company of squirrels. Students on the verge of final exams and summer freedom milled about. They wore shorts and tank tops, book bags flung over their shoulders like afterthoughts. Frisbees whizzed through the air.

"So what are you planning on doing after graduation?" I asked, once we were settled on the grass.

"Well, I've written a bunch of poems. I'm going to try to get them published."

"Wow." I took a sip of coffee. "You're so different from what I expected. I thought you'd be harsh and cynical like Maggie and the rest of them, but you're a poet."

Noel shrugged. "I'm *trying* to be a poet. I'll give it my best shot and if I don't make it, at least I'll know I tried."

My mind flashed to Miguel. He'd been a gifted musician, good enough to make a living at it, yet that hadn't been enough. What would have made him decide to live, I wondered. Not music, not me, not the baby that grew and grew. What then?

"And you?" Noel asked. "What's your consuming obsession? What do you want to be when you grow up?"

I could have hugged him for not looking at me and thinking "welfare mother" or "what a shame." I leaned back on my elbows, squinting against the sun. "I've always loved water. Maybe I'll be a wreck diver like my great-grandmother."

"Cool. Or you could be a marine biologist."

I'd never thought of that before, but it didn't sound too bad.

We stayed out on the lawn until shadows lengthened and Noel looked at his watch. "Oops! An hour and a half past my break time."

He promised to bring the guitar to me soon, and I promised I'd be waiting.

Actually, I wasn't there. I'd taken to roaming. I was trying to retrace Miguel's steps. I walked slowly, sweat running down my legs. My feet took me down tree-lined streets, through neighborhoods where pig-tailed black girls twirled ropes in the street. I returned to the house one afternoon and found the guitar lying on Miguel's bed, the bed I'd slept on since his death. Fragments of a poem were woven through the guitar strings.

The ghost of Miguel did not sing, did not play for me.

One afternoon, two months after that night, that train, I walked down to Five Points. I went to the music store next to the gourmet shop with its sidewalk tables and fresh coffee smells. A little bell tinkled when I pushed open the door. The interior was a little musty. Dust had collected on organ tops. Classical music played softly. In the background, there was another sound—the soughing of sand on wood. Soon, that sound ceased and a bespectacled young man appeared. He held a hunk of blond wood in his hand. On closer inspection, I saw that it was a musical instrument. This man was a craftsman.

"It's a mandolin," he said, noticing my interest. "I sell them at fairs."

I was impressed and said so, but I wasn't there to buy a mandolin. "I need a book," I said. "Something to teach me how to play the guitar."

He smiled broadly. I suppose he was amused at the unlikelihood of an egg-shaped girl like me taking up such a hobby. Wasn't I supposed to be learning how to change diapers? And shouldn't I be craving dill pickles instead of Gypsy guitar music? Nevertheless, he showed me to a rack of books and recommended two or three. I bought a couple and went back to the house.

"You like to drive me crazy with all that strumming,"

Maggie said after a couple of weeks of my chord progressions.

I'd developed blisters and calluses on my fingertips. I'd mastered A, F, and G minor, and their simple sounds were as beautiful to me as any full-fledged melody.

Maggie and I were getting on each other's nerves. Without Miguel, we didn't have anything to tie us together. Neither one of us wanted to sit around rehashing that night by the train tracks.

I took my guitar out to the stone steps and started playing "Proud Mary." It was the first song I'd learned. I warbled along, oblivious to the paperboy delivering the afternoon edition and the neighbors watering their lawns.

My concentration was intense, solely on frets and chords, leaving no room for the putt-putt-putt of a Volkswagon Beetle. The engine died and a car door opened and slammed. I looked up and there was Noel.

"Hi," I said. "I guess I owe you money."

He grinned. "Play me something and I'll call us even."

"I'm not very good. I just started."

He sat down beside me.

"So what happened to your band?" I asked.

"We're still playing. I got another guitar. You wanna join?"

"Right." I laughed. "Like this?" I pointed at my big belly, my swollen ankles, and my fallen-down socks.

"You look great," he said, a little too seriously.

I couldn't meet his eyes. He reached over and pushed a wisp of hair behind my ear. Then he traced my jaw from earlobe to chin. I felt sparks jumping along my spine, dispersing among nerves. I wanted to, quick, turn my head and bite his finger, just to connect with someone warm and whole.

With a feathery touch, he guided me toward him. My mouth wanted his so badly that I couldn't stop it from opening, kissing, sucking, tasting his tongue. He was strawberry-and-cigarette flavored, and I'd never tasted anything so delicious. A thousand horses galloped in my chest. Then, Noel pulled back and studied me like one of his rare books.

"I've wanted to do that ever since the first time I saw you."

"Me, too." Saying it, I knew it was true.

We sat there through the long afternoon and into evening, watching the cars go by. All the while I was thinking, "This is the love I could have had," and, "Oh, how uncomplicated happiness can sometimes be."

Summer came. My stomach was as big as a watermelon. The heat was heavy and sticky, making the slightest movement a chore. I wanted only to lie under the ceiling fan and let myself be hypnotized by the rotating blades. I propped my bulging feet on a soiled throw pillow and breathed the soupy air. If I were in Grand Haven right then, I would be lying on a beach while the gulls dipped and glided above. All the left-behind comforts rushed into my mind—that clean, soft bed next to Amanda's, the plush grass beneath bare feet, the cool water my sister and I drank from the garden hose. If I closed my eyes, I could almost hear the bees buzzing among tiger lilies and roses and daffodils. Even the memory of discomfort—the slivery wooden bench I sat upon while watching the pastel spurts of the musical fountain or the jostle of shoulders and elbows as I made my way among carnival booths—brought on a pang of longing.

For the first time in my life, I knew what it meant to be landlocked. The ocean was three hours away. I couldn't see the waves or smell its briny perfume or dip my feet into its healing waters. It might as well not have existed at all.

Though the locals went to Lake Murray for fishing and waterskiing, to me, it wasn't a "real" lake. I had spent my life near a freshwater sea. A body of water one could cross by boat in a matter of minutes was a poor substitute. How could I dream about the gray docks clinging to the opposite shore? How could I conjure sea creatures and sunken chests of jewels?

I was homesick.

In coming all this way, my troubles had not abated, my problems had not been solved. Sorrow had deepened, and I knew now that it would be never-ending, but alone, in that hot, humid place, I lacked strength and courage. There was nothing for me there. It was time to go back.

26

The music was as familiar to me as my name. First, soft yet powerful chords, then the slow crescendo leading to drumbeats with an insistent tribal rhythm. There was such majesty, such drama. I always pictured giant icebergs breaking off into the Arctic sea, or mountains, just as immense, rising above me, dwarfing me, leaving me breathless. When I'd learned that the theme song had been borrowed from a movie—*2001: a Space Odyssey*—I'd been a bit disappointed. But nothing could disassociate that music from the spewing columns of colored water.

I sat on the wooden bleacher, a backpack with my few clothes and the guitar in its case beside me. I was surrounded by strangers. Grand Haven was a small town and I'd expected to be bumping into friends and acquaintances left and right, but so far, I was sunk in anonymity. I ignored the other spectators and concentrated on the water, plumes of pink swaying in a graceful ballet.

I'd been to the Musical Fountain show many times and I'd always loved it. Seeing it now restored something to me. A sliver of peace lodged in my brain. The music and water lulled me, hypnotized me.

A few boats were anchored in the river just in front of the bleachers. Passengers in captain's hats sipped pop and watched the show. From a little ways off, carnival sounds drifted over. During quiet moments, I could hear the merry-go-round tinkle, the snap of pop guns.

I wondered if Amanda was there. She'd be with a band of friends—cheerleaders, dancers, the future home-coming court. Or maybe she had another boyfriend by now. I could picture some hunky guy tossing rubber rings at Coke bottles, trying to snare a stuffed panda for my little sister.

Did she miss me? Had she taken over my half of the closet, appropriated my records and the funky rhine-stone jewelry I'd accumulated from visits to Kiki's Closet? Knowing her taste, she'd probably donated all my stuff to the church white elephant sale. Or maybe the family had held a garage sale—payback for the check I'd forged. I figured I deserved no less.

Tears pooled in my eyes, and the blues and pinks of the water, now fanned out like a peacock's tail, blurred together. I blinked to clear my vision.

"I did it because of you," I wanted to say to my mother.

A vision of Mom on her knees, mouth twisted, her whole body stunned by betrayal, jumped into my head. I'd grown up hearing about her could-have-been life, a bus ticket in a drawer haunting me like a ghost. I'd done it so that I would not feed on the bitter dregs of regret for the rest of my life. There was no right or wrong path, I wanted to tell her. There were only decisions, choices made, and how we deal with the consequences.

But look at me. What were my choices? My baby had no father to look after it. My money was all gone. I had no means of looking after a child. I could go home, but then what? Would my parents take one look at me and shut the door in my face? *Okay, Great-grandmother Margaret, tell me what to do. What would you do?*

When at last the water subsided, I remained in the bleachers until all the others had filed out. I disregarded the anxious and curious expressions of the tourists who squeezed past my knees. I knew I looked a little rough. My hair hadn't been washed in three days, and my clothes were stained with truck stop ketchup (I'd had an accident with a sandwich back in Tennessee). What did I look like to those strangers? A demented young transient? Or a young woman at peace?

To tell the truth, I was somewhere in between. I got up from the bench and started walking. At first, I thought I'd go in the direction of the marina where pleasure boats were moored for the night. I'd always loved reading their fanciful names—Meredith's Folly, Dara's Dream, Sea Fairy. As a child, I'd tried to puzzle out the sources of inspiration. But on this night, there were likely to be people about. They'd be partying on houseboats, sprawled over decks with cases of beer. The town was mid-festival, and there was probably no quiet nook for me to hide in and nurse my wounds. If I couldn't have solitude, I wanted water. I started walking to the beach.

As soon as I reached the sand, I set down the guitar and my backpack, took off my shoes, and stepped onto the silky dune. I scuffed through sugar to the edge of the water and stood still while the waves licked my ankles. In the shallows, the water was blood warm. Ahh, my lake. I wanted to drink it up. It occurred to me that all the answers to my questions were in this lake.

The moon glowed up above. Its reflection undulated with the waves. The stars were so bright and clear they seemed graspable. Farther down, a pair of lovers were out for a moonlit stroll. I watched their progress, made clumsy by their bumping hips, made slow by their frequent embraces. I thought of Miguel, and then Noel, their images alternating like spliced film clips. I thought of Miguel at the Ferris wheel and that motel room in Chicago with its water-spotted walls and his fingers as they'd plucked guitar strings. I tried to block out the railroad tracks, that last horrible vision.

I sat down on the sand and sifted crystals through my fingers, my hand an hourglass. How much time did I measure? Before I knew it, the couple was gone. The road beyond was without cars. I was completely alone.

I decided to walk to the pier. The big red lighthouse sent out its beacon. I hadn't seen any boats for hours, figured only phantom fisherman were likely to heed the signal. I walked all the way to the end, my feet still bare. The concrete was rough and cool on my soles.

When I reached the edge, I sat down and let my legs hang over. Waves broke against the pier, spraying my skin. I stared into the night—nothing but black water and black sky. I listened to the waves rising and breaking, the gentle wind entering my ears like whispers. At first, just whoosh, whish, but then, "Eli-s-s-se. Eli-s-s-s-e." A breath, a caress. "Eli-s-s-se. Eli-s-s-se." And it came to me little by little that I was hearing not wind, but the voice of the water. It was calling my name.

My knees pulled up, my hips scooched back. I leaned on my hands and pushed myself up.

"Eli-s-s-s-e."

And I saw not dark mystery, but comfort, liquid arms reaching out to catch me, a mouth to swallow my misery. I dove into the water. I dove and the undertow held me fast, secure in its embrace. My limbs were limp, unresisting. Bubbles floated from my mouth. My eyes were open, but I saw nothing. Only black, black, black. Then, there was no more air and I opened my mouth to breathe. Water rushed in. I started choking. My hands clawed at the wall of water, but the lake's muscles tightened.

Drown. I was going to drown. I kicked and clawed

and spun in the water. I didn't want to die. I hadn't known it until that very moment, but now it was as clear as the sky way above.

And then, as if my wish to live had beckoned her, I saw a mermaid. She was large and strong, her muscular tail glowed phosphorescent in the dark water. Her face was as pale as pearls, her mouth a slash of coral. Her eyes were the exact color of the water, gray and surreally transparent. Her hair was green, amorphous, and like a seine, caught everything in its path. Minnows and sunfish and baby salmon swam among the strands of her glorious tresses. As I watched her approach, I forgot my struggle. Will gave way to wonder. I was too preoccupied to consider why she had come, like an angel of the deep, to loft me through fathoms. Together, powered by her fabulous fish tail, we rose through water, to the surface, and I sputtered back to life.

EPILOGUE

"Here she comes!" my mother's voice tinkles. She is as bubbly as Lawrence Welk's ballroom. She stands beside me, scarved and wearing sunglasses. Dad raises his camera just as the float comes into view. And then there's Amanda, looking like a bride on a cake, gliding down Main Street. Her crown is slightly askew, and I check an urge to clamber aboard and straighten it.

Little scab-kneed Margaret is entranced by an ant.

"Look!" I say. "It's Aunt Amanda! It's Miss Coast Guard!"

My Gypsy child starts waving at the beauty queen.

The local newspaper made much of multi-generational beauty. "Dynastic dreams," someone wrote. "The crown is passed on." A photo and an article of Mom and Amanda took up half a page. There was much reminiscing on Mom's part, and bright predictions for Amanda's future. No one mentioned, of course, the wayward sister and daughter, mother of Margaret. That's okay.

I imagine if the committee knew half the things I know about my sister, they wouldn't have crowned her, but I'm not one for spilling. I am not the one who broke a sisterly confidence on Valentine's Day two years ago.

Little did I know, there was a PI on my tail. I hear the snoops were drawing near. They'd gotten as far as

Georgia, I later found out. But I was back on a bus by then.

My mother said it was the Coast Guard who saved my life. I don't believe her. I didn't see those white uniformed men she spoke so highly of. I recall no boat. I remember only water, and then a white-walled hospital room.

When I came to, I was tucked into crisp white sheets and a plastic bracelet encircled my wrist. Mom held my hand in both of hers and her face was the first thing I saw. I thought for a moment that I'd woken from a long dream. Like Dorothy, maybe I'd been roaming the land of Oz and the past few months had never really happened.

There was a sweetness on my mother's face. My eyelids fluttered and I felt her hand on my forehead, smoothing back my hair. Where was the murderous she-devil I'd expected? Why was she being so nice?

I looked down at my stomach, now deflated. I felt a soreness there when I lifted my neck, but the baby was gone.

Mom noticed my puzzlement and said, "She's fine. Your baby's fine. The doctor cut her out this morning."

I lay back in the pillows, overcome for a moment by the prospect of motherhood. I had no clear image of what was to come. It was more like fear mixed with wonder. I was a *mother*. M-O-T-H-E-R. I opened my parched lips and said the word out loud.

"Yes?" Mom thought I was talking to her.

I rolled my head from side to side. No, no. I was too weak and confused to sort out the jumble of thoughts in my head. I was drugged, too, though I didn't realize it till later. I'd been under anesthesia during the emergency C-section.

"Mermaid," I managed to get out. "Long green hair."

Mom brought my hand to her mouth and kissed it tenderly. "Hush now, dear. You need some rest."

Chiara, looking great with a bob, came to visit the following afternoon. She'd changed her style from bohemian to something like a forties screen queen. She wore a long dress in a post-WWII floral print. She was visiting her grandmother for the summer.

"My mother's in town, too," she said. "But I'll wait till you get your strength back before I spring that woman on you."

She told me she'd sworn off booze, but now she was addicted to caffeine. She drank three cups of coffee during our visit. Mom wouldn't allow me any, saying it was bad for my milk.

I told Chiara about my search for Miguel, and how I'd wound up sitting on the edge of the pier. I even told her about the mermaid.

"That sounds like a great story," she said. "I think I'll write about it in my next novel."

She laid the thick manuscript of her first on my nightstand. It would give me something to do while I was stuck in bed.

"By the way, your baby is beautiful," she said. "A keeper."

Yes, I kept her. Yes, she is beautiful. She has eyes like coal that smolder whenever she is angry. She does little flamenco steps when she doesn't get her way, which isn't often. My mother, who must remember her lost child, gives Margaret everything she wants.

In naming her, I was hoping to bring my great-grandmother into the fold. I'd like to think that we can all forgive her now. That once unutterable name, is now spoken at all hours. Margaret, Margaret, Margaret.

I've given her a middle name, in honor of her father. It's the one thing that I wanted to give him: Hope.

CPSIA information can be obtained
at www.ICGtesting.com
Printed in the USA
LVOW08s1703090217
523759LV00003B/749/P